Out of the Blue

Out of the Blue
New Short Fiction from Iceland

Helen Mitsios, Editor
Foreword by Sjón

University of Minnesota Press
Minneapolis
London

"Killer Whale" by Ólafur Gunnarsson was first published in English in *The Thaw* (New American Press, 2014).

Published by the University of Minnesota Press
111 Third Avenue South, Suite 290
Minneapolis, MN 55401-2520
http://www.upress.umn.edu

ISBN 978-1-5179-0253-7 (hc)
ISBN 978-1-5179-0233-9 (pb)

A Cataloging-in-Publication record for this book is available from the Library of Congress.

Printed in the United States of America on acid-free paper

The University of Minnesota is an equal-opportunity educator and employer.

22 21 20 19 18 17   10 9 8 7 6 5 4 3 2 1

Dear friends, let us not worry about literature.
It will live on. We will die.

—Steinn Steinarr, Icelandic poet

Contents

Foreword
Four Fragments from Reflections on Icelandic Narrative Arts

SJÓN

I

UNTIL 1971, it is said, Icelanders were strangers to the field of human inquiry that seeks to know the self and analyze reality, otherwise known as philosophy. When, in that year, teaching in the subject was introduced at the University of Iceland, it was taken as a sign of pandering to the hippie generation's penchant for idleness and trouble making. The first teachers of philosophy were seen as eccentrics—even more eccentric than psychiatrists—and many years passed before they won recognition for themselves and their subject.

Hitherto, schools of thought grounded in classical rhetoric, which required coherent (not to mention logical) argument, were anathema to the Icelanders, who dismissed them as mere hot air. Those of their compatriots who had been duped into studying such things at foreign universities—to which they had been sent to learn something of practical use—were quickly weaned off the

IX

habit when they returned home. They were loaded with tasks that kept them too busy to think and thus spared from becoming an embarrassment to themselves and their families. The odd individual got away with practicing philosophy under the guise of aesthetics or psychology, though these subjects were also regarded with suspicion, especially psychology. Theology, in contrast, was thought to contain no philosophy at all, its practice the sole province of clergy and the occasional lunatic. Indeed, the bitter religious schisms that split the Icelandic community in North America were held up as evidence of the dangers inherent in trying to interpret the Bible instead of simply reading it as a rollicking tale. The same applied to political ideologies: they were the hobbyhorses of loudmouths and self-seekers who were apt to ruin confirmation parties and Christmas festivities with their wrangling. One of the few groups to get away with a type of discourse that smacked of philosophy was the Theosophical Society, but as theosophy was enshrouded in Eastern mysticism and appealed almost exclusively to well-to-do Reykjavík ladies, little attention was paid to its teachings. Because Icelanders made no distinction between philosophy and cosmogony, the theories of the geologist Dr. Helgi Pjeturss (who posited the existence of a material afterlife on distant planets connected by an astral force called the beam of life) were long hailed as Iceland's only native school of philosophy.

II

IN PLACE OF PHILOSOPHY, the Icelanders had poetry and tales. If the ultimate questions of existence were to be discussed in all seriousness, this was best achieved, it was felt, through the swapping of this type of offering. Debates on the interaction between body and soul, for example, could be conducted through the medium of verses or stories about birds. The meaning was often a trifle obscure, but as it was up to the audience to divine the parable from the contents and then respond with offerings of their own, the process could result in dialogues that were felt by all to shed light on the matter—although to the uninitiated it might sound as though their talk was going everywhere and nowhere at once.

The first speaker might open the proceedings as follows:

"The soul, now, there's an odd beast."

Then embark on an account of the Golden Plover, which, instead of migrating south in the autumn, overwinters in Iceland, flocking in caves, where it hibernates with a leaf in its beak. Should one stumble on such a place, where the birds lie scattered over the floor of the cave, their eyes closed, breasts rising and falling in sleep, one must never remove the leaf from the plover's beak. To do so would kill the bird, and this evil deed would call down lifelong misfortune on the culprit.

The next speaker might feel moved to recite the opening stanza of a poem about a moonbeam by Hulda, alias the poetess Unnur Benediktsdóttir Bjarklind, which is rendered as follows in Skúli Johnson's translation:

If the moonbeam,
Airy and bright,
Feathers possessed
And the power of flight:
On his pinions of snow
I would ask him to go,
O'er ocean and land
At my love's command.

The third speaker—unable perhaps to remember anything of interest about birds just then—could easily steer the conversation down a different path, recalling instead an incident that took place on the farm of Hrafnagil, or "Ravens' Gully" (his contribution justified, of course, by the reference to birds in the name). At Hrafnagil there once lived an old woman whose sight was growing dim. One day, when the parish priest was expected to call, she peered down over the hayfields in the hope of seeing him arrive. A stallion happened to be mounting a mare at the time. The old lady remarked:

"The man of God's slouching in his saddle today."

This too could help to illuminate the image of the soul. And now the discussion could really take wing.

IV

IN THE BEGINNING WERE THE EDDIC POEMS. They begot the Skaldic Verses and the Sagas of Icelanders. . . .

When foreign readers open books by contemporary Icelandic authors, they automatically compare their contents to yardsticks that do few people any favors. Modern writers are drafted in as proof that eight hundred to a thousand years ago there arose from the mingling of Norse and Irish cultural roots a world-class literature in the Icelandic tongue—though this ignores the fact that already by the fourteenth century the ever-scribbling Icelanders had frittered away the knowledge that had led to the creation of these great works. For the next four hundred years, the only works of narrative fiction produced in the country were those that vagrants could carry from farm to farm in their heads. There, they were transformed into metrical ballads, which, along with gossip and "plain-speaking" verses, served as social currency in those days. The purveyors of these ballads, or *rímur,* received payment in food and lodging. They were sometimes praised but more often met with contempt. Meanwhile, officials compiled annals and reports. Men of science wrote descriptions of natural history. Eccentrics collected all kinds of texts, both instructive and idle, in handwritten commonplace books. And priests composed sermons.

By the eighteenth century, so completely had the Icelanders lost touch with the tradition of writing narratives in prose that when Eiríkur Laxdal returned home from Copenhagen, where he had encountered the latest trends in European literature, none of his countrymen had a clue what he meant. Still less did they appreciate that his manuscript, "The Saga of Ólafur Þórhallason," contained a novel that in its structure and artistry recalls the Polish count Jan Potocki's masterpiece, *The Manuscript Found in Saragossa*. Count Potocki shot himself with a silver bullet in Podolia, in the belief that he was turning into a werewolf; Eiríkur Laxdal, brought low by all-too-human flaws, ended his days as a beggar, and his great novel was not published until 1986. It still remains almost entirely unknown and unread.

Then, on April 23, 1902, Halldór Guðjónsson was born, in Reykjavík. After taking the name of Laxness for himself, he became invincible. And there you have the difference between "ness" and "dal."

VII

PERHAPS IT IS BECAUSE PHILOSOPHY REACHED these shores comparatively late that Icelandic writers have never felt bound by the truth. While recognizing no literature except that which springs from reality, they reserve the right to distort the truth according to the demands of their tales. And the same, naturally, applies to all that has been written above.

Translated by Victoria Cribb

Introduction

HELEN MITSIOS

WHEN I FIRST VISITED ICELAND in the 1980s, I felt I had landed on a magical island. It was unlike any place I'd ever seen, comprising a countryside of benign fairy-tale charm as well as bleak highlands of sparse trees—a kind of *Waiting for Godot* stage set of volcanic rocks and craters where one could easily imagine ghosts, trolls, werewolves, and other creatures of Icelandic mythology lurking about. Here, people were named after Nordic gods from one of my favorite childhood books, *Children of Odin* by Padraic Colum. Nowhere have I felt more air-dropped into the land of Viking sagas. Nowhere have I been so reminded of our earth's churning center, from the sulphurous water that poured out of showerheads to the misty geothermal hot springs of Reykjavík's enviable public swimming pools, to the natural wonders of the active land of Haukadalur "park," where geysers spout into the air. But I'm hardly the only enthusiast of Iceland, for as I write this Introduction it is projected that this year an estimated 2,000,000 tourists will visit the small island of around 331,000 inhabitants nudged under the Arctic Circle at 66 degrees latitude and about a six-hour flight from New York.

Fast-forward many years after my first visit, and I'm still besotted with the country: its people, the geography, the hint of the supernatural in the air, and particularly the literature. Short stories are an Icelandic tradition. With the first settlers about 1,100 years ago came the tale, the short story, and the legendary saga. Storytelling in its various iterations became a permanent medium of exchange between people, for Icelanders, even to this day, are forever telling tales and short stories to amuse each other. On a daily basis, the short story is more like an anecdote, but it can surface when you least expect it and become a tale about the various experiences of fellow travelers, deadly serious or gleeful gossip, or respectful or envious relating of the good fortune of others.

This regard for entertaining conversation (and the oft-mentioned fact that Icelanders read and write more books per person than do inhabitants of any other country) marks the island as a special place. The love of telling tales, and of reading and writing, creates a fertile ground for highly imaginative writers whose natural ease in storytelling underscores their superb talent. Like the lyrics of a good country-western song, the stories in this collection touch on primary themes of human nature: love, hate, identity, jealousy, revenge, betrayal, honor, and tradition. The stories explore a wide range of subjects and states of mind, from a modern retelling of a Nordic saga to a tale with Ingmar Bergman-like psychological interiority to the nautical theme of a killer whale and the ever-prevalent wine-dark seas (if I may borrow a Homeric tag) at the juncture of the North Atlantic and Arctic Oceans.

When I visit Reykjavík from time to time and talk to my writer friends, I often feel as I did during my undergraduate college days at the English department of Arizona State University, discussing books with the passion and gravitas I had when I first discovered that literature has the power to change a person's life. I still believe it has this power. I entreat you, dear reader, to decide for yourself, and I welcome you to the wondrous landscape of twenty Icelandic short stories that might spur your wanderlust and take you on adventures that touch both your heart and mind.

Out of the Blue

Self-Portrait

AUÐUR JÓNSDÓTTIR

A WEIGHTY SWELL, the screeching of children tickles her ear canals, along with the breaking waves that foam on the seashore. She can't quite believe she's lying on a sunny beach in Sardinia, the scent of sunscreen in her nostrils, the taste of salt on her lips. But that's what's happening, after years of dreaming sun-warmed seas. The distant sound of terrible music reaches her ears, buzzing in a strangely comforting way: somewhere, someone is listening to tinny pop through headphones.

She opens her eyes and immediately squints at the fierce light. Before her stands a man she can perceive only by his outline reflected in the sea. She struggles to open her eyes wide to get a better look.

The man contrasts the sky, a stripe in limpid blue. Dark-skinned and with a striking posture, he stands there with the sea behind him. In his right hand he holds a cooler with a blue lid; he's stacked ten or so pink-ribboned straw hats on his head. He's hawking cold drinks and sun hats. His voice is deep, low, and musical, almost seductive. Sweat drips from his pronounced features; he looks around blankly, the whites of his eyes bloodened.

"Mom, aren't you going to buy something?" she hears from somewhere beside her.

"No," she says, hearing herself force her voice to sound neutral.

"But can't you see how tired he is?"

"If I buy from him, I'll have to buy from all of them."

"All who, Mom? He's the only one."

"But then he'll tell the others. Tell them we're buying," she repeats, automatically using the same tone as Gunnar Bjarni had when he used the same phrase to her, almost word for word, earlier that morning while the kids tiptoed screeching across the hot sand wanting to buy some ice cream from an ice cart, burning their soles on the way. She pretended she was looking intently after them while he said the beach was swarming with all sorts of salesmen; she must avoid eye contact with them like wildfire.

The salesmen were wearing long robes, either white like a cloud wisp in the sky above, or else brightly colored and forming adventurous patterns. Some sold drinks, others hats, some beach towels or skirts. The past few days they had hardly been able to open their eyes without pushy salesmen looming over them, so they'd resorted to going further up the coast, where there were fewer people and consequently not so many hawkers.

"I'm going to buy from him all the same! I'll pay you back at home, Mom."

Fríða rushes over, grabs the beach bag, and roots about for euros; in a blink she's already bought both a straw hat with a pale pink ribbon and a cold can of orange soda. She sets her hat on top of her thick golden locks and smiles, beautifully olive-brown, freckles on the tip of her nose. Then she opens the can with a loud *hviss* and tilts her head. "Take a picture of me, Mom!" she commands, posing sweetly.

She indulges her daughter. She reaches for the phone that has drifted deep into her beach bag, underneath underwear, kids' sunscreen (SPF 50), and tanning sunscreen (SPF 30); she brushes the invisible sand off and, smiling, tells her daughter to smile. The smile broadens even further across her face.

"Let's both be in the picture!" cries Fríða. So she leans over to her daughter, feels her hot, fragrant skin up close, and smiles into the device alongside her.

"Cheese!"

. . . .

"Where did you get that hat, Fríða?"

"I bought it."

"What were you thinking?" he asks, directing his stare at her instead of the culprit, their daughter. His voice is affronted, some would say contemptuous.

"I wasn't thinking anything," she says, frustrated. "Fríða just bought a hat."

"You have to have some control over her." He snorts at her before looking back at Fríða and saying, exasperated, "Fríða, this is about as smart as taking a sugary doughnut into a field in August."

"What do you mean?" She asks it so innocently that it borders on provocation.

"I mean just what I say, sweetie. If you take sugar into the sun, wasps will come."

They look silently at him, resting there, sure of himself. He has the same golden shine to his hair as Fríða, his face sunburned but his body white in his red swimming trunks; he has a broad chest and athletic feet in leather beach sandals. He loves us, he's just tired of having to take care of us all the time, she thinks to herself, admiring her own ability to mediate.

"There, there, my little ladies, don't be upset. I just have to watch you so we don't end up broke," he says, changing from his previous joylessness and looking affectionately at them.

"Of course we're upset. You're comparing the poor guy to wasps!" says his daughter angrily.

"No, baby, he wasn't saying that, not exactly," she hears herself saying. "He was just . . . yeah, just, of course we want a little peace here. There's someone constantly trying to sell us something."

"Yes, listen to your mother, my darling," he says distractedly, heading fast toward the sea and shouting, "Tommi, come on, you can't go out that far!"

He turns back to them and says, "Listen, let's ask these women to take a picture of us when Tommi comes out. I've always wanted a picture of us all together on a sunny beach. What about you, Sigga?"

"Yes," she says in an empty voice, watching her son break through the waves and up out of the ocean. "Absolutely, babe."

She wraps a towel around Tommi's slender, wet body as he exaggeratedly chatters his teeth and Gunnar Bjarni rabbits in broken German to the women under the next umbrella; they respond positively to everything he says, laughing with pleasure at being able to do this favor. One is tall and thin in a neon-green bikini, the other a little plump and wearing a peach swimshirt. Both from southern Germany, they say, both with hats they bought from the salesman after chatting flirtatiously—but still patronizing him.

A moment later they are sitting close together. She with Tommi in a towel between her thighs, Gunnar Bjarni with one arm around her, the other down around Fríða, who covers her bare breasts with a towel and faces the camera grumpily.

"Cheese!"

....

"It's an offensive sales pitch to tell people the beach is within walking distance of the city center," announces Gunnar Bjarni so loudly that people at the bus stop look at him, though they don't understand the words. Italian housewives with tired but happy children, hungry salesmen who have dragged across the sea from Africa and who sit on the roadside in the fleeting shadows of dry bushes.

She keeps quiet, though she agrees with him. She would never have come if she'd known. What? she asks herself. What could I possibly have known?

She doesn't have a chance to answer herself, because Tommi needs to pee. He grabs at his crotch and looks beseechingly at her.

"Not now!" she sighs. The bus is approaching at speed, at long last, after forty minutes of their waiting under the scorching afternoon sun. If she takes him aside, they'll definitely miss the bus, which is usually so packed that they feel like sardines in a can, people having to press themselves up against one another just so the door can close.

She trusts neither Gunnar Bjarni nor Fríða with Tommi in the crush. On the way out to the beach, she'd kept a strong hold on him, making sure not to lose sight of him, to risk his being washed away in the crowd at the wrong stop. The stops are surprisingly scattered along the route. It's at least a thirty-minute journey to downtown, if the bus doesn't break down like last time—then the trip could be twice as long.

She feels dizzy, the afternoon temperatures up to unbearable on this never-ending traffic island along the dusty highway where they all loiter, facing several houses with shuttered windows, houses sheltered by high walls. They have to take great care not to stumble into the road.

People congregate around the bus like a fat snake when it stops. Gunnar Bjarni and Fríða thread skillfully through the crowd, although they're bulging with beach stuff: an air mattress, towels, buckets and shovels, sunscreen, an umbrella, swimwear. They rely on her to get Tommi and herself into the sardine can.

"I need to pee!" he wails.

"Not now, Tommi. You'll have to hold it."

"But I'll pee myself!"

"No, darling, you must be able to hold it," she says while picturing him urinating on himself in the throng. Better that shame than waiting for the next bus, exposed to 104-degree heat.

In the same breath, she feels his hand slip from hers; he slides past countless butts and thighs, away from the children in this sweaty lather of people and up to the nearest bush.

Fear grips her like ice crystals around the iced girl in his favorite movie, *Frozen*. A surge of adrenaline propels her past men and women; she bursts through a stream of pungent, thick bodies and finally escapes out to Tommi, who is standing happily, peeing a river on the dead bushes.

"Sigga!" she hears Gunnar Bjarni shout, so loud that his voice cracks with anger and despair. Too late. The door closes on him as he stands behind what must be two rows of sticky human beings smudged together in the heat. The bus drives off. They stand there, together with several salesmen who couldn't fit on.

"Mom! What are we going to do?" cries Tommi, widening his eyes at her as soon as he hurries to fasten his shorts. He gestures dramatically, exaggeratedly, hardly able to conceal the exhilaration that it's truly exciting to lose his dad and Fríða, to be alone at a bus stop in a foreign country.

"I don't know," she says, out of habit.

She can't think straight in this heat. The next bus isn't expected for another forty minutes at the earliest, and there are no taxis on the motorway. She has Fríða's cell phone in the beach bag, but it has an Icelandic SIM card, and when she tries to call Gunnar, she gets in touch with an Italian woman's voice saying something she doesn't understand.

"Mom!"

"Yes, baby."

"Take a picture of us! So Dad and Fríða can see us lost."

He looks expectantly at her, laughing despite everything, and strokes his hot head. Tufts of light hair, stiff from the sea salt and sand, above bright blue eyes that are always fraught with excitement, no matter what.

"Yes, why not?" She feels she's having difficulty talking in the heat. "If you put on your sun hat."

"Okay, Mom!"

"Okay. Are you ready?"

"Yes."

"Cheese!"

....

Gunnar Bjarni had said something on their very first day here about the Mafia presence on the bus system. She had barely paid attention, was just vaguely aware of some hoarse muttering along the route they took to and from the beach. Now she was pretty convinced he had the right idea. There's no sign of the next bus. Mist rises at the end of the road, a transparent fire. The cars that rush past and whirl up dust are passenger cars, trucks, or tourist buses.

Time stands still. They've long ago finished the contents of the water bottle, and spendthrift Fríða had used the last coins in the beach bag when she bought her hat and soda. Sigga decides she'll have to sneak them both onto the bus, providing it actually comes. After all, there's no possible way anyone could work out who in the whole barrel of herrings has paid a fare.

"Mom, I'm thirsty."

"I don't have anything more to drink, baby."

"But I'm dying of thirst," says Tommi, weakly though theatrically, taking himself by the throat and sticking out his tongue.

"You have to wait," she says, becoming stubborn. Why hasn't Gunnar Bjarni come back in a taxi? He's obstinate. But Fríða? She imagines Fríða verbally haranguing him to call a taxi or . . .

"Perdono!"

"Ha?"

For the second time that day, she looks into those eyes with their bloodshot whites. This time the glance isn't neutral but filled with sympathy. The man smiles kindly as he stretches his face, and his high cheekbones tauten as he says, "Your boy! Water? Aqua?"

Tommi is the first to answer. He practically snatches the bottle from the man's hands and gulps down water. He emits animalistic moans between swigs of water and reacts reluctantly when she tells him that's enough now, he can't finish the man's water. She returns the bottle and smiles feebly in gratitude. The man laughingly waves the bottle away, opens the cooler bag, and dishes out a can of orange soda. That perks Tommi up, but she stirs herself to say, "No, no!" and opens the beach bag to show that there's not so much as a single euro lurking inside.

But the man continues to smile, like they are all having fun together, and extends the can to Tommi just as before.

"Okay, madam," he says, and pats Tommi on the head. "Little boy drink."

And so her little boy does, feeling light and carefree as the afternoon sun gets hotter with every minute that passes.

Before she knows it, she has to explain their problem in fragmented phrases in English and three Romance languages. She hears Gunnar Bjarni's imagined warnings and turns a deaf ear to them. He would probably tell her not to be so trusting, alone on a trip with a group of strange salesmen who are desperately seeking their unlikely fortunes. Something, yes, any something that would give them enough to feed themselves and their families—perhaps the three women and a group of children who bed down in a train station and live in secluded garden plots.

His companions crowd together: seven dark heads, one striped tee and six robes in colorful patterns that call to mind both animals and nature, seven deep voices. Two of them have mobile phones; they both try to call the number she gives them, but without success. On Fríða's phone, the same incomprehensible voice as earlier can be heard saying something she can't understand, never mind what the woman is trying to explain.

She would dearly love to lie down on the ground, let her eyelids droop, and run together with the heat like a person who wants nothing but to submit, to become one with a snowstorm. But Tommi is with her. She's got to find a way out of this before he becomes so giddy that he wanders out into traffic, unaware of himself.

"Look what the man gave me!"

"What, baby?" she asks, blinking rapidly.

"A friendship bracelet, and look, he put three animals on it. A lion, see, a frog, and also an elephant."

He stretches out a chubby, tanned arm. Around his wrist is tied a colorful string from which hang three tiny silver animals.

Tommi smiles like the sun and looks happily at one of the salesmen, a man shorter than the other, stouter, with a boyish face and playful gaze. He winks at her inscrutably, and she gets embarrassed. He finally looks away when another man comes over and announces something that makes him sigh heavily and wave his hands in front of himself. It's like they've gotten bad news.

"Madam, you come with us? We walk. To the city," asks the graveled voice; the reddened eyes look questioningly at her.

"No," she says, nervously giggling as she makes it clear that mother and son will wait for the bus.

"No bus."

"No bus?"

"Not today," says the man, and explains that his acquaintance has gotten wind of an unexpected drivers' strike.

Her life seems to have transformed into a nightmarish farce. How can it be that mother and son are standing here, forgotten, in this absurd situation? Was Gunnar Bjarni right when he said that the public transportation here was unusable?

She has long been unable to protest everything he makes a fuss about. It's all just wind past her ears; she usually waits for him to settle down, to submit gradually like a baby with an upset stomach, smiling furtively at him—except when she begins to choke up, which happens sometimes, and then she has to step aside.

The heat escalates her blood pressure and melts her patience. Maybe she's starting to get sunstroke: a steel-cold hatred tenses her body and winds taut. In a dreamlike heat-haze, she suddenly loathes herself for always being ready to bolt. Cornered in a life that could be so good but somehow isn't. These strange emotions seem more real than anything else. She will not break down. She's going to hate on; she's going to find a way out of all this.

"Come on, Tommi," she says icily. "We're going to walk back into town with these men."

"Does Dad know?" he asks, hesitant.

"I trust them more than your dad," she says, knowing that at some time she'll have to ask Tommi's forgiveness for the unwarranted discomfort this remark will cause, in so many ways. For now, there are only two options, and if she doesn't leave this place, she'll die. That much she knows.

"Mom!"

"Yes?"

"Will you take a picture of me with the men? So Dad knows they saved us."

"Yes," she says, while Tommi bounces over to his companions, who have begun to gather their baggage.

"CHEESE, Mom, cheese!"

"Cheese!"

....

She follows at a distance and watches as her son bows over the head of the tall man who carries him on his shoulders, as light-footed as he is earnest in his eyes. The white cowl moves in the sorely missed half breeze that bolts away like a mouse. The sandal on her right foot hurts her heel, but she won't risk stepping out of the sandals for fear of treading on broken glass or dead insects along the desiccated roadside.

The men are quite different from one another. The broad-shouldered one seems at ease, and the tall one is amused; the others are less aware of the two of them, with the exception of a young, agile man, the only one wearing jeans and sneakers, who looks steadily at her and briefly looks ahead when she meets his eyes.

She takes care to look in another direction, and suddenly they are under a bridge with the highway over their heads. The sound of the road is reminiscent of a huge river in thaw, but the stink of piss is too pungent for her to breathe properly. They see no one there except some drunks, who crouch noddingly against the brightly colored, graffitied wall.

What could she be thinking, rushing out into this unknown with Tommi? They are completely vulnerable with these men. The men could grab hold of her and rape her in front of him. Kill her and sell Tommi to pedophiles. Had Gunnar Bjarni also been right the time he said it was just speaking plain to say some women had only themselves to blame for being raped when they got themselves into perilous situations?

He will scold her for her actions later, if she gets out of this alive. So what? He's constantly grumbling about things.

And Fríða scolds him. And they harangue one another until she joins in the game and says something that causes them both to mock her.

She walks fast and stares at Tommi on the man's shoulders as though a glance can ward off any risk he faces.

Sometimes, she wishes her family were more like her workplace. The hospital ward where she tends to patients: there, it's enough to show you care. There's no need to complicate matters. All that's right in the world stems from one person tending to his or her neighbor. She never feels stupid, lame, or out of touch, the way father and daughter so often seem to see her. There, people consider her a complete woman with a solution for each of them. Of course, the patients are quite different from one another, and there are lots of them. But among them she can be herself.

The patients see it, she says to herself as they step out of the bridge tunnel and find that the bright light hurts their pupils. They see this woman, the one sauntering along the highway now, watching her half-asleep son lolling about on a stranger's shoulders.

This woman must be homeless, she imagines the people think who rush past in air-conditioned cars. If, that is, they pay her any more heed than the next palm tree, having long since become impervious to all the homeless people wandering the streets. Though she is light skinned. That's curious, perhaps. A light-skinned woman and her boy hanging about with a group of dark men.

Their first night in the city, as she stood on the street, she saw something white stirring in the night. Something like a spirit seemed to hover in the gleam of the dull lamps on a narrow street leading down from the mountain. When it drew near, she saw that it was two men in white robes. They were so light in step they didn't seem of this world. As they turned into a room that lay opposite one door, a dwelling reminiscent of a cave, there came a sweet smell of well-spiced food. She heard the hum of many voices, an infant's crying.

Her head is unbearably hot. She grabs Fríða's sweaty T-shirt and ties it on her head. She inhales the sea air along with the highway pollution and smiles to herself. Despite everything, it all feels just about bearable. All around are mountains and the sea and nature. Like in the Westfjords when she was a teenage girl, wandering around with older boys and sneaking off to light a cigarette and sip on something stronger, something that made her love one of them in a whole new way.

That was the life waiting for her, and she was more than willing to step into it, whatever country it was, to march forward in a gloriously careless blindness. Like now, perhaps, she thinks to herself, giggling nervously and surprised to find herself longing suddenly for a cigarette after eighteen years of abstinence. She hasn't smoked since she became pregnant with Fríða and lost the right to her own body.

Fríða had smiled with all of her body at a young man who tried to sell her both jewelry and himself on their second or third night in Cagliari.

"Don't be so dumb, Fríða," her dad had told her, merrily tipsy after half a bottle of red wine and a shot of grappa. "He's like that with all the girls."

"You don't know anything."

"I was a boy once."

"So what! Did you start going with Mom because she was the only one who liked you?"

"They all wanted me."

"And maybe this boy has a crush on me. Perhaps it's love at first sight!"

"Don't be so naive, my dear."

"You don't be such a caveman."

"Look there."

"At?"

"There on the wall, Fríða. What's been graffitied on it?"

"'Nous' . . . I have no idea."

"'Nous vous haïssons.'"

"So what!"

"'We hate you,'" her dad said. "That's what it means, in French. You should know that most of these boys come from the former colonies of France."

"What should I know?"

"Ask yourself," he said smugly as Fríða sauntered off, turning up her nose at them, though she stopped and peered at the words on the ancient wall, which gleamed yellowish in the streetlights. This city was already ancient by the time the Romans built their lair here. Various populations had taken it off various others since long before Christ. Long before it became a custom to set images of the Virgin Mary on rock ledges, surrounded by candles and incense, like the ones highest up on the corner of the building closest to the wall.

A loud honking from a commercial truck startles her from her thoughts. Suddenly, they have come a long way; she has floated along as if she were in a dream or delirious from the heat. Walking without noticing her steps, not even her painful heel. She needs to pee but can't ask them to stop. Tommi seems to be asleep on the man's shoulders.

Six days ago, she left her home in Reykjavík, on Grafarvogur. Made sure she'd locked it and set the burglar alarm. As she closed the front door, she felt a certain regret. Standing there, outside, a coziness to looking around, though it was still just August; for a moment, she was more tempted to have that cozy home be their long-awaited family vacation spot rather than rushing off somewhere because Gunnar Bjarni had chanced on some cheap airline tickets. If she'd only known she'd never return home.

She's no longer the person who left; she can't see home the same way again. "I have no home," she whispers into the hot breeze, which wafts the words out into the world. Before she knows it, she has come to a stop, fished the phone out of the beach bag, and pointed it at herself.

She's never paid attention to her own image, but suddenly she finds she's taking a picture of herself.

"To orient myself," she says, surprised at a strange element in her voice. She tucks her hair around her ear and whispers breathlessly: "Cheese!"

....

The police were bound to stop them. It wasn't right, the authorities felt, a light-skinned woman and a light-skinned boy wandering the city with a group of dark-skinned men.

To her indescribable relief, the men pretend not to see her saviors; they are allowed to continue their journey, bearing their packages, without intervention. She sees them turn the corner. They have arrived in the city, and from here she needs to find her way to the guesthouse up the mountain.

But she's without a key and must somehow get hold of Gunnar Bjarni and Fríða.

The officers are kindly but paternalistic, acting like they've just rescued her from serious peril. They joke with Tommi, tousle his hair, say how cute his mother is.

It's a relief to sit in an air-conditioned police car. Tommi is excited, recently awake and in high spirits after all the adventure. She answers in monosyllabic words, trying to say as little as possible, realizing that in some perverse way she would have liked to continue being lost.

The police are taking a well-put-together, smiling woman in a beautiful summer dress under their wing, helping her make a call.

Gunnar Bjarni answers, sounding a little shaken. "I was so scared!" he says quietly. "This isn't like you."

"Me!" she exhales, but decides to say nothing further. She says nothing, either, when he appears in the doorway with their daughter, red-eyed, at his heels.

"Tommi!" Fríða shouts out, hugging her brother, though his dad has the boy's undivided attention.

"Look, Dad! Mom and I were lost and gone!" says Tommi, rushing into his arms, brandishing the cell phone. On the screen is a picture of him with a group of men who wave enthusiastically at the phone, like they want to send the whole world a cheerful greeting. He's seated on the shoulders of the tallest one, who narrows one of his eyes and smiles at the woman with the phone.

"A wonderful picture," says his dad, confused, and looks at her as she smiles. What else to do? They're on vacation.

"Now we've got to get ourselves a decent bite to eat," says Gunnar Bjarni, grabbing Tommi to him and hugging all of them in his long, thick arms. Pressing her to him so the kids are crumpled between them. He is so consumed by sentimentality that she feels his breath rising up his nose and struggling out into the heat. Her world is still all in one piece.

"Pizza!" cries Tom.

"Pizza and ice cream," chimes his dad, drying his watery eyes with his palm. "Because I love you so much."

Translated by Lytton Smith

Afternoon by the Pacific Ocean

KRISTÍN ÓMARSDÓTTIR

O NCE, AS SHE HAD MANY TIMES BEFORE, Greta Garbo went to visit her colleague Marilyn Monroe on her home turf, the City of Angels. Greta, who lived in New York, flew over to the West Coast of the United States and took a cab at the airport over to Marilyn's, who received her like only she could, barefoot in a housecoat. She often had an apron on, because she loved to bake bread rolls for Greta, who ignited such passion in her for bread rolls. Greta said she often had this effect on people. They wanted to bake for her and feed her delicious gourmet foods. Marilyn Monroe agreed, because she had never before or since had any interest in baking rolls for anyone else. She did enjoy pulling the cork out of a wine bottle among good friends, especially to divert attention from herself. But Greta didn't have a demanding presence. She was aloof and distant and, always tired after a flight, lost herself in looking at details in the environment: a statue of a naked pugilist with a towel around his neck, a clear ashtray reminiscent of an aquarium, the book on the coffee table.

As is well known, Greta and Marilyn had been avid readers ever since they were little girls, one in Los Angeles and the other in Stockholm, and they had cultivated quite a taste. Literature and bread rolls united them. Marilyn offered Greta champagne, which she accepted if the visit fell on a Saturday. Few things were more Saturday-like than champagne after all the Saturday brunches between the wars. And now there was world peace, although she had forgotten nothing and so many had perished. She would never stop mourning, but sparkling liquid sparks a tired psyche.

"How many years are there between us again, dear Marilyn?" asked Greta, holding a glass of champagne in one hand and leafing through *Ulysses* by James Joyce with the other. This was a new commemorative edition, with a lovely typeface, great line spacing, and a super-cool cover.

"Oh, I don't remember," lied Marilyn, who was very good at memorizing dates, years, and birthdays, as she glazed the bread rolls with egg whites. It was rare that she forgot long-lost friends' birthdays or birthdays of those she had not broken up with. She couldn't help it. Her memory never failed her, and Greta had asked that question countless times before, and just as often received the same answer, "Oh, I don't remember," in an innocent voice.

Then she slid the baking sheet with the bread rolls into the oven, closed the oven, pulled off the oven mitts and removed her apron, poured champagne into a glass, and walked over to Greta, who was sitting on the only chair in the living room with *Ulysses* on her lap.

Marilyn said, "There are about twenty-one years between us."

"Yes, that's right," said Greta, and not for the first time. "Was I twenty when you were born?"

"And how old will you be, dear cinnamon stick, when I die?" asked Marilyn sweetly and with obvious glee.

She touched the movie star's shoulders and started kneading them.

"Oh, cut it out, Marilyn," Greta replied in a deep voice. "Don't be so melodramatic."

"You remind me of a morose Swede," she added.

Then Marilyn laughed out loud, because she adored looking like a morose Swede. It connected her orphan heart with a vague origin, a Norwegian father she didn't know. The two actresses looked at these common roots to Scandinavia as a solid connection, but they pooh-poohed all drivel about the origin of the species, nationality, and families.

"We're free beings in a borderless world," hissed Greta once in the face of a chain-smoking Danish journalist who had conceived a notion of their friendship and wanted to interview them for a nationalistic Danish newspaper in a series of articles about Nordic beauty.

"Beauty connects us," said Marilyn to the Danish guy, "our inner beauty."

Now, she rubbed Greta's shoulders and asked, "Can you smell the baking aroma?"

Greta nodded.

"Don't you think I'm so matronly and nice to you?"

Greta nodded.

"I want you to have motherly feelings toward me."

"I do," said Greta. "I feel like you are my American mother."

"Good," said Marilyn and thought to herself, American mother—a great title for a poem—tomorrow I'll write a poem called "American Mother."

Then she stopped rubbing her friend's shoulders, kissed her on the back of the neck, tiptoed over to the oven, tied the apron back on, put on the oven mitts, opened the oven, and pulled out the baking sheet with the aromatic bread rolls.

Greta opened her gold bag, which was a small valise designed for trips that wouldn't take her away longer than one night from home; there, she kept a small travel-size toothbrush, a small tube of toothpaste, pajamas, a scarf, two sets of underwear, two pairs of pantyhose, a small deodorant spray can, a vial of perfume, a washcloth, a small towel, and *Egil's Saga* in an English translation. She picked up the book and put it on top of *Ulysses*. Marilyn turned around and smiled.

"Don't you love this aroma?" she asked.

"Yes," said Greta as she closed the bag and walked over to Marilyn.

Together they moved the bread rolls from the baking sheet over to a cute plate that they had bought in Mexico on one of their trips.

"The aroma of the bread rolls fits perfectly with the aroma of you," said Greta.

"Yes, I'm wearing the perfume you gave me, Acqua di Parma."

"Good," said Greta. "I so love it when my gifts are useful."

Marilyn kissed Greta on the cheek and said, "You are so sweet."

Then she took off the apron and the oven mitts, and took the Mexican dish with the bread rolls into the living room. They sat on the floor as though at a picnic, but the floor wasn't green but a rather sand-colored carpet, wonderfully soft to the touch for barefoot women like them. Greta, wearing loose work pants and a silk top, folded up the pant legs like sturdy men do at a picnic. Marilyn put her hair in a ponytail. She yawned and said something about always being so sleepy.

"Ditto," said Greta. "If I'm not sleepy, then something is wrong."

They ate a few rolls and washed them down with the champagne. Greta rolled over on her stomach and stretched out to her full length. Marilyn lay down on her side in the fetal position, and with one hand under her cheek, she looked wide-eyed at Greta, who opened *Egil's Saga*. They were at the part where Egil wants to marry Asgerdur after returning from a successful raid. Greta started reading with Marilyn watching her. The sun over the Pacific pierced through the curtains of the big window and bathed the actresses' feet in golden rays. Greta is a wonderful reader, thought Marilyn, and Greta felt the same thing about Marilyn.

When the day waned and the rolls had been consumed, they left the living room.

In the bathroom, which was covered in pink tiles, they took off their clothes and changed into pink-and-green pajamas, washed their makeup off, and brushed their teeth. Then they went to the bedroom.

They continued reading in bed by the light of a lamp above the headboard.

"Good night," said Marilyn.

"Sweet dreams," said Greta.

Translated by Sola Bjarnadóttir O'Connell

Escape for Men

GERÐUR KRISTNÝ

H ERE, IT IS NEITHER THE TRAFFIC DIN nor the noise from the market that wakes me up. It is the odor. It's a mixture of car exhaust and the cologne that Frikki bought at the duty-free. Escape for Men.

I get out of bed and glance through the window. The owner of the café lines his chairs up on the sidewalk. On the other side of the trees, street vendors spread out their goods. It must be Saturday. Then it is three days since Frikki decided to vanish. At first I thought he was kidding when he grabbed his gym bag with his stuff and said he was out of here. I just said OK and continued drying my hair. Half an hour went by before I realized he was gone. I went out and looked for him in the dark, but the search yielded nothing but an old lady who yelled at me when I tripped over her dog. However, the dog didn't mind at all. Just thought I was playing with him.

I went back up to the room for a few minutes. Then I decided not to let this nonsense ruin my vacation. Mainly, I am used to traveling alone, and, second, Frikki and I have been together only for three months, so this was not entirely a surprise. Perhaps it was just my own thoughtlessness to go on vacation with Frikki, but it just so happened that the short time fate had allotted us also spanned my vacation time.

I don't even know why he wanted to come with me to this place. Well, he knew van Gogh once lived around here. He had a poster of the sunflowers in his kitchen, and that is why he wanted to see where van Gogh had been. Then, when I dragged Frikki to the Chagall Museum, he had no interest in the art on the walls and strode impatiently through it. He was more fascinated with the water lilies on the pond in the garden. What else can you expect from a political science major?

It wasn't until yesterday that I understood why Frikki left. On the train from Paris, I was telling him about when I was an exchange student here and couldn't avoid mentioning the boyfriend I had then. Paul. I haven't heard from him in the ten years that have passed since. I was considering whether or not to contact him. Just to be polite and, of course, out of curiosity.

Frikki pointed out to me that perhaps Paul has a girlfriend who has no interest in my knocking on their door. He meant, of course, that perhaps I have a boyfriend who is not interested in my reviving old love. Imagine being in love with someone I haven't seen for so long! I can barely remember what he looked like—except those heavy eyebrows that met above his nose and those dark eyes that could make me do all kinds of things. We even replicated the butter scene from *The Last Tango in Paris*. It would have been more French to use La vache qui rit spreadable cheese. Today, I can say "Paul" a hundred times without my nipples getting hard. But then again, I can also say "Frikki" a hundred times and not notice any bodily changes.

When we arrived at the guesthouse, all was forgotten. We started out by laughing at the tired face on the Saint Mary icon in the hallway, then we laughed at the acid pattern on the wallpaper in our room. We wondered what those brown streaks were on the bathroom tiles, and, after seeing the towels, we thought odds were they had been used to stem blood from gunshot wounds.

Frikki has never been to France before, and he thought everything was just great—the food, the people, the paddleboats. He even befriended the boring boys with the ghetto blaster who played loud music for the entire beach without being asked. For the few days we were at the beach, we were drowning in techno-pop. The boys obviously liked the song where a man shouts "Ecuador!" with the enthusiasm that only a South American immigrant pining for home can muster.

On the third day I started wondering whether Paul still lives in the same place. I said I was going for a walk the following day to see if I could find the house where his family had lived. Frikki said I could go without him. That wasn't news. It had always been my intention.

I called out to him from the bathroom, where I was blow-drying my hair, that I just had to give Paul the pleasure of seeing if I had changed, and to tell him I had stuck to my plans of owning a flower shop when I grew up. That was when I heard Frikki say he was leaving. He forgot his cologne. It sits on top of the giant wardrobe in the corner of the room. The hotel wallpaper hanger obviously couldn't budge the wardrobe from the wall when he repapered the room, so he just papered both sides of it.

It's best to go to the beach in the morning and spread out before everyone else arrives. I put on a blue cotton dress, tie my hair in a ponytail, and put on sandals. I greet Rosa, the woman at the reception, but dash out before she has a chance to look up. It didn't take her long to notice I was suddenly alone, and she's asked me twice where my handsome boyfriend is. I pretend not to understand.

At the market, lace tablecloths for sale are all jumbled with lavender soaps and chocolates. Few things seem to have changed since I was here last. If it weren't for the incessant pings and rings from cell phones, it would practically be the same. I always feel embarrassed when I see people walking around talking loudly on their phones. I think phone conversations are too private to be yelling into the wind. One might just as well walk around in public with a toilet to the rear end.

I should have left earlier. The beach is already crowded with tourists, and most of them sound German or Scandinavian.

I spread my towel on the sand and sit down. I am careful to apply sun protection. If fashion magazines are correct, then there is nothing more dangerous than sun rays. Seventeen-year-old boys with brand-new driver's licenses are nothing in comparison. Then I lie down with a summer-vacation book about the growing problem among British women, according to contemporary literature: breast-feeding while wearing a Prada suit.

The Norwegians next to me tell stories about more realistic problems. They are so fat that they could easily get jobs with the harbor council as buoys. One story is about a wedding that the most handsome of these guys attended. He was sitting next to his buddy and spoke at great length about how ugly the mother of the bride was. "I said she looked like a pig, but didn't know she was sitting right next to me."

They laugh and shake like jelly on a plate.

There is little breeze, and it is as if the lapping waves and the people noise keep growing louder. I have a headache. I put my book down and try to relax. It doesn't work. The pain increases, and soon enough nausea rolls over me so that I drag myself up and head back.

Back at the hotel, I run right into Rosa. She notices right away that I am ill and tells me that I must have sunstroke and that I should always wear a hat while outside. Too late to tell me now. It seems to me that Saint Mary has a new look on her face, a shadow of a smile, but perhaps it's just a "who's-tired-now" look.

Six-story guesthouse and no elevator. I manage to get up to my room on the fifth floor and kick off my sandals before throwing myself on the bed. A fly is stuck inside the light shade. Its buzzing sounds like a jackhammer.

It wants to escape the heat.

I want to escape the heat.

After a while I dream I am at the dentist.

I'm startled when there is a knock on the door. I have slept so deeply that it takes a while for me to know where I am.

Rosa is outside the door, decked out with at least ten plastic bracelets in colors like M&Ms. She asks me if I'm feeling better.

I tell her I am. The headache has turned into a soft throb. Rosa announces that tonight there will be a party for sixty people at the hotel, but it should neither keep me up nor slow my healing, because she is giving me a bottle of aspirin. I accept it and express my gratitude. I barely close the door before I have to run into the bathroom and throw up. Afterward I feel somewhat better. I fiddle around until evening, give myself a manicure, rub conditioner into the cuticles and apply hardener.

When night falls, I discover that aspirin isn't curing my headache, which is only growing stronger once the party starts. It doesn't matter that it's several floors below. The big band that plays on the beach at night has been hired to entertain the partygoers. The sound is wafting through my window. Perhaps Rosa meant I should chew the pills and then stuff them in my ears. I mull this over while I continue reading about the woman who has one child but many suits.

The following day, I buy a red baseball cap with a picture of Lucky Luke. I feel good as new and want to go on with my vacation. I head out to the old part of the city. By the harbor a man is selling tickets to Corsica. I've never been there. I am in the middle of inquiring about prices when I see a barbershop and fish shop standing side by side on the other side of the harbor. I suddenly remember where Paul used to live. I thank the ticket man for the information and dash off. Past the store where the ice cream cones are locked in a freezer outside the shop and you have to ask the saleswoman to come out and open it. Past the bakery, where the owner's son (incapable of dealing with me without throwing in sexual innuendos) works. Seems like a severe case of Tourette's syndrome, but it certainly has increased my French vocabulary quite a bit.

Paul's house is just as I remember it. White and surrounded by shrubbery. A girl playing with a dog is in the yard. When I approach the gate, the dog runs toward me, barking happily. It is missing one ear.

"Come here, Vincent," yells the kid, and the animal obeys. She glares at me angrily and says, "This is my dog."

On one of the gateposts is a family name, but it doesn't sound like Paul's family name. I also don't recognize the curtains I see in Paul's window. His were white.

I pull out my camera and snap a picture of the house before continuing on. I don't get far before the little girl yells after me, "Money, money, money."

They don't have to be grown before learning how to speak to tourists. She will clearly go far in life. Not sure about the dog.

I follow the path that Paul and I used to take to school, and take a shortcut through a backyard to avoid the big road. Paul used to go ahead of me and help me climb the fence. Just as I swing over the fence, I notice the surprised face of a woman in a window of the house next door. People are probably not used to seeing a thirty-year-old woman leaping over fences.

Summer break, and the school is obviously empty. Vacation does not, however, prevent some kids from taking full advantage of the basketball court. Boys are jumping around with a ball. I want to have a picture of me by the old school. I walk over to the boys and ask one of them to take a picture of me. He happily agrees, and I pose by the steps. The boy tells me a few times to move back just a little, and I obey. When there are about five meters between us, the boys run off with my camera. Clearly a well-rehearsed move.

I feel the anger bubble up in me, but try to look on the bright side. Now I'll have a lighter load and don't have to constantly spend time taking pictures. I'm finally feeling angry at Frikki for having disappeared; otherwise he would have been the one taking the picture of me.

Oddly, this is not the first time I have been robbed while on a trip. A transistor radio vanished from a beach in Portugal, and some hotel maid fell for the temptation to snatch my lingerie from a hotel in Oslo. We must have been the same size. I thus know from experience that in order to be reimbursed by travel insurance, I have to file a police report. At the police station a blond woman around fifty receives me and neatly types my story of the bad boys. Actually, I just have to say a few words before she accurately takes over the narrative. One would think she had been there observing in person, but she probably just heard this story before. I ask whether I should leave both my home and hotel address if the camera is returned. She looks at me blandly and tells me that nothing that disappears here ever comes back. Behind her I spot a poster of little girls with the tagline "Have you seen her?" I realize a stolen camera is not the worst of what this woman has to deal with.

I'm barely out the door when a young man pops up and asks in English if he can shoot me. I am startled and look around for someone to help me get away from this lunatic. I ask the man why he wants to shoot *me*. He replies snarkily that this is an American expression and points at his camera. I yell at him to leave me alone and march off with his inquiring face looking at my back.

I have dinner at a pizza place and use the time to write some postcards to my parents. I don't mention the runaway boyfriend or stolen camera. After dinner I take a walk. It never seems to be dusk here. Darkness falls like a theater curtain, and people immediately rush to the streets. The old millionaire hotels invite their guests to parties at private beaches. Kids pop up on roller skates, and a jazz band steps onto a stage that's been raised on a sidewalk next to the beach. The big band is careful to maintain a proper distance.

I constantly have to step out of the way for couples. It's as if they think it's equal to signing a divorce agreement for them to let go of each other's hand in order to let poor singles like me pass by. This gets to be tiresome, so I head for the hostel. I am also hankering for a shower.

The hostel is on a street where there's one Asian restaurant after another. Some windows have interesting displays, and in the Filipino one there is a huge aquarium. I stop to admire the colorful fish. I'm counting the different varieties when I notice a familiar face in the restaurant. If it isn't the damn boy who snatched my camera, sitting there with his girlfriend like nothing happened.

My stomach feels a funny tickle. Oh no! On the table between the happy couple is today's loot—my camera. I comb my hair with my fingers and put on some lipstick. Then I march into the restaurant. I greet the host and tell him I'm with the people at the other end of the room. I walk to the boy's table, grab my camera, and tell them that it's my property. He doesn't seem to recognize me and smiles nervously at his girlfriend. I speed out of there, but he suddenly gets it and follows me and asks, "Who do you think you are?" I always consider that to be private information and don't reply. He grabs my shoulder and seems ready to fight. Without thinking, I pull my keychain out of my purse and hit the boy in the face with the keys from my flower shop, my parents' house, my house, my bicycle, and my storage room. Then I ask him if he wants me to shoot him. Without waiting for a reply, I snap a photo while he's running away holding his bloody nose. One for the grandkids.

Rosa asks me cheerfully, as usual, if I slept well in spite of the party the night before. I lie and say I slept like a baby. She gets me to help her hang a map of the area on the wall. I notice a town I've heard of, Arles. I've never been there.

The train swooshes by one sunflower field after another. This is a summer of drought, and the irrigation systems spray water halos over the fields.

When I get out of the train station, I aim directly for the old town, which is surrounded by a wall. I buy a map of the place at the first shop I see. Then I go to the Roman Theater and check on the acoustics by reciting a few stanzas from *Guide to Christian Living*, by Hallgrimur Petursson. When a group of Dutch schoolkids storm in, I head to the arena, where the odor of dung left over from

the latest bullfight lingers in the air. The acoustics are undoubt-
edly better here than in the theater. I situate myself in the middle of the arena. I wait a short while in case a charging bull will
suddenly appear, but they're probably kept elsewhere when not
being tortured. Then I start again with *Guide to Christian Living*.
Quietly at first, and then gradually increasing the volume so that
my voice fills the whole arena. The tourists are surprised but then
obediently sit down and listen. They probably think the town's
entertainment committee has hired me to amuse them. I abandon
the *Guide*. Suddenly, I think I hear my name being called. A man
appears, running down the aisle. Frikki. So this is where he's been
hiding. Do I stay mad at him and pretend I don't see him, or be
nice and show him that his disappearance hasn't bothered me at
all? I pick the latter and wave to him.

Frikki jumps down to me and asks, "What the hell is the meaning of all this howling?" I ask him in return, what was the meaning
of his disappearance? He doesn't reply directly, but says he came
here because van Gogh used to live here, but his house was blown
up a long time ago. I ask if the artist survived the blast, but Frikki
says he was long dead by then, as the house was blown up in the
war. Then he says, as if nothing has happened, "Let's go."

We fetch his bag from a nearby hostel and then meander along
the river until the train leaves. I tell Frikki about the boy who stole
my camera and what happened when I found it again. Frikki says
I'm nuts, but he laughs, so obviously he doesn't really think so. I'm
careful not to mention that I went to the house where Paul used to
live. Frikki doesn't ask about that anyway. When we get back, we go
to the newsstand at the train station, where I buy a copy of *Elle*. As
I hand a bill to the vendor, I notice out of the corner of my eye that
someone is watching me. I look aside and see the observer looking
back down at his newspaper. Frikki is absorbed in trying to pick a
snack and hasn't noticed anything. I look at the man again and for
a brief moment our eyes meet. There is no doubt. The eyebrows
meet right above the rim of stylish glasses. I smile and he does, too.

I'm mulling over what the next step would be when the vendor interrupts me.

"Aren't you going to take your change?"

I apologize and pocket the coins. When I turn around again, Paul has sat down on a bench. Right next to him is a trash can. I walk over and toss my train ticket and whisper, "Wait a little bit."

He nods.

Then I walk back to Frikki and tell him to hurry. He pays for his snack and we walk out together. He drapes his arm over my shoulder and tells me he's taking me out to dinner this evening. We rush to the hostel. Rosa is thrilled to see Frikki again. Her non-stop chatter almost prevents us from reaching our room. She tells him he missed a great party, as if she'd intended to invite only him and not me.

I make sure to shower before him. When I'm dressed and tie my hair up, I spray a tiny bit of his cologne on me. Then I wait until I hear the shower running. I tell him I just have to pop out for a minute, and he says OK. The Saint Mary icon in the hallway spreads her arms toward me.

Translated by Sola Bjarnadóttir O'Connell

The Most Precious Secret

EINAR ÖRN GUNNARSSON

1

THE DIRTY PANELED WALLS OF THE CAFÉ were covered with paintings by one of the regulars, who was better known for his avant-garde poetry and out-of-control drinking. The artworks were painted in bright colors, and upon careful examination sex organs could be seen in all of them. Their frames were made of knotty pine, and the signature reached halfway across the canvas.

Ómar sat alone in a corner, in torn jeans, a shabby threadbare sweater, and a heavy, matted wool coat with untrustworthy pockets. His filterless cigarette was old and flared brightly as he took a drag. A tall young waitress with long red hair leaned leisurely against a wooden pole and stared absentmindedly at the dark street outside. After a while she noticed him but was in no hurry, since service was incidental at this restaurant, where the worn carpets were saturated with the odors of smoke and stale beer.

A long time passed, after the girl took his order, until a cup of coffee appeared on the table. The cup's rim was chipped, and its saucer was cracked.

He frequented this place, the Blue Elephant. He usually had black coffee during the day, but on weekend evenings he brought a small flask to dilute it.

He lifted the cup slowly to his lips and looked around in the vain hope of spotting someone he knew. No acquaintances were around, so he finished his coffee and sauntered out into the night. He stopped at one bar after another, but wherever he went, no one had a spare minute for him. Deep down he felt like a ghost roaming a party town.

In his heart he often cried and longed to die and be relieved of the painful burden of being a daily witness to how cruel life can be to delicate dreams.

A few years ago he was a superman who despised the masses and their notion of work. For him, even just one of his paintings had more to do with life than all the world combined. He read in his brushstrokes the same genius displayed in the works of Braque, Munch, and Klimt.

Ómar had graduated from the Icelandic Art Academy with excellent grades and headed to Copenhagen, but in spite of his talent was unable to find any work except cleaning offices and drawing unfunny cartoons for trashy magazines.

As he stood in a bar listening to a stocky girl sing "Strange Fruit" in a deep voice, a woman came up to him and asked him for a light. She was about fifty, thin, with dyed black hair. When he lit her cigarette, he thought about how bizarre she looked wearing clothes that were suitable for a teenager—red jeans and a black blouse tied just above her waist, exposing her belly button. At first, she seemed shy and standoffish, but when they started talking about painting, he sensed a strange inner beauty emanating from her words and her almost enchanting way of speaking.

In her sea-green eyes was a hint of primal energy, which he later realized was just painful loneliness. Time flew by during their exciting chat about art. She was an ocean of wisdom, and when she mentioned particular artists, her spirit was on fire.

Just as in a third-rate movie, they were so immersed in their conversation that they didn't notice the place had closed, all the lights were on, and the waiters were busy stacking chairs on the tables. When the waiter asked them to kindly leave, Ómar surprised himself by inviting her to his place.

As they sat in his studio sipping red wine, she told him a story about a girl who had left Denmark for Spain and married a wealthy Catalonian man. When her husband died of old age, she returned to her childhood homeland. Together, they had traveled the world. Her life was a strange adventure.

Ómar listened to this lively story and avoided dragging out his own dreary one. As luck would have it, Frank Sinatra's voice suddenly came wafting down to them, giving him opportunity to tell her about his neighbor Jörgen, a man who had inherited a fortune but wasted every penny.

Every time Jörgen lost his faith in life after long drinking sprees, he listened over and over to the song "My Way." Sometimes he invited Ómar over, played the song, and asked him to translate the lyrics so that the cathedral choir could sing it in Danish at his funeral, which he was sure was right around the corner. Jörgen often cried when he described how sad the mourners would be. "This is the story of my life," he used to say. "I always went my own way."

She laughed, and he felt as if something came to life deep inside him. It was like a thick lump had been dislodged in his heart.

When Gitte asked to see his latest painting, he was evasive at first but eventually caved in to her pleading.

"Your paintings are so special. You paint differently," she said contemplatively. "There's incredible energy in your works. The colors are so unusual; they have mysterious, enchanting hues."

Although Ómar felt a certain pride, he took her words with a grain of salt, mindful of life's hard lessons. By morning she had selected two paintings that she said she was determined to buy, whatever the price. She asked him to bring them to her that evening.

2

ÓMAR STOOD IN FRONT OF HER HOUSE with his paintings in his hands and a bouquet of roses squished under his arm. Leading up to the big, stately house was a long, well-lit path.

As soon as he touched the doorbell, which was also a security camera, a bright white light flooded the yard. The door opened instantly. Gitte greeted him in a low-cut red dress, wearing makeup and looking dignified.

Ómar brought the paintings into a huge living room.

Upon seeing the masterpieces that hung on her walls, he was filled with terrible insecurity. For a second, he felt like grabbing his paintings and running for the door, but then he heard Gitte's voice enthusiastically praising the unfathomable energy in his paintings.

"You remind me sometimes of Antoni Clavé." She placed the paintings under those of the Catalan master.

"I see the same spark in your works," she said. "There's that dark surface, but somewhere behind the gloom are joy and endless creativity. I knew Clavé personally. He often looked as if he were suffering from the effects of self-destructive urges—but it was quite the opposite. To anyone who managed to get close to him, it was clear that Clavé was joy and lust for life personified."

Ómar said nothing, but deep inside he agreed that the paintings were somewhat similar.

"You're the best-kept secret here in Copenhagen," she said. "I must have more of your paintings."

They removed several large oil paintings from the wall and hung his in their places—where they looked quite good. Ómar had never imagined that his paintings would ever grace such an elegant living room. Gitte was excited, nearly intoxicated in her admiration. "You've got to put yourself out there. You can't just sit there waiting in your studio for the world to knock at your door. You've got to attract the world's attention to yourself. . . ."

Gitte gave a long, encouraging speech, and the longer she went on about his works, his boundless creativity, and his limitless talent, the more a deep-rooted faith in his own ability grew inside him. Before, he'd always called his feelings of inferiority by other names, such as humility, timidity, and shyness.

He relished listening to her and found it amazing how she could go on and on. In the middle of her speech, she suddenly walked up to him and kissed him passionately. In his heart, he'd been longing for just that. He kissed her back and felt that the kiss was the start of something new. Around midnight, they went to the bedroom and enjoyed what the night had to offer, and there were many more nights to come.

3

WEEKS AND MONTHS WENT BY. They could hardly ever be apart. Everything he said was admired, and even the silence that sometimes rose between them wasn't really silence but an opportunity to bask in each other's adoration. Gitte was relentless in her encouragement, convincing Ómar that the future was his, especially if he continued to develop the windmill theme that he'd spun out from a painting by Piet Mondrian. He painted every day, and with all the encouragement, ideas began taking shape in different ways. For the first time in years, he felt the unstrained energy inside of him. His creativity was at an all-time high, and his self-confidence grew with each new piece. Gitte was with him in the studio, sharing in his newfound, radiant aplomb. Once the day's yield had been signed, in big letters, they'd walk around the city holding hands, visiting the National Gallery of Denmark, eating at the finest restaurants, or gallery-hopping. No opening that mattered passed them by.

One day, when Ómar was painting to his heart's content, Gitte showed up at the studio with a distinguished older gentleman. When the man held out his hand, it dawned on Ómar that this was

Mr. Larsen, the owner of Gallery Z on Gothersgade, the most prestigious art gallery in Copenhagen. Ómar had brought his portfolio there once, but an assistant had turned him away at the door before he even had a chance to introduce himself to Mr. Larsen. To Ómar, that visit to Gallery Z was one of the most humiliating moments in his career. The assistant had asked Mr. Larsen if he wanted to look at the portfolio, but Larsen, annoyed, stood in his office doorway and said so loudly that it echoed through the showroom, "I don't need to see it; I can tell immediately from people's eyes and demeanor whether they're artists or not."

"Ómar," said Gitte cheerfully, "this is Knud Larsen, an old friend of mine. I ran into him by accident at the Hotel d'Angleterre. We haven't seen each other for many many years. I forced him to come here and insisted he take a look at your paintings."

It was obvious from the look in Mr. Larsen's eyes that he had absolutely no interest in the visit, but once he saw the first painting, he was eager to see more.

"Have you made plans to show these works?" asked Mr. Larsen, barely able to take his eyes off the paintings.

Before Ómar could even think of a reply, Mr. Larsen eagerly asked, "You're preparing for an exhibition, I suppose—but do you have a contract?" Mr. Larsen lacked the words to describe the choice of colors, the form, the wealth of ideas.

"Why haven't you ever come to see me, boy? You're a major talent," he said.

Ómar felt an urge to be honest and remind Larsen what he'd said about the eyes and demeanors of talentless people. But he repressed the urge. It probably wasn't a good idea to be resentful.

"I've been charged with arranging an exhibition at the Spanish Embassy to commemorate Saint George's Day," said Mr. Larsen.

"It's a big day in Catalonia, especially in Barcelona," injected Gitte. "Xavier and I used to go out early in the morning, walk around the city, and not get back until late at night. There's such a wonderful atmosphere on Passeig de Gracia and other streets.

The bookstores have stalls out on the streets, where they sell books at half price. Everyone gives their loved ones a book or a rose on that day. Darling, we should go there sometime and give each other flowers and books."

"The windmills in your works really spark my interest," said Mr. Larsen. "As you know, April 23rd is the day Cervantes died, and Shakespeare, too, come to think of it. It's the day of living and dead poets. It's like your windmill series is tailor-made for such a commemorative exhibition. I can well imagine that crazy Don Quixote seeing them in the same way."

4

THE ART CRITIC KNUD SØNDERGAARD, an older man with a bald spot surrounded by a ring of white hair, a well-known snob, elbowed his way around the gallery, spilling people's cocktails as he went along, scribbling notes about each painting. Ómar felt a shiver but thought he should say hello to the critic. Just as he was about to do so, Gitte grabbed his arm and whispered that he'd better not, because it might be interpreted as kissing up to him. Suddenly Mr. Søndergaard took a few steps back, scattering the people behind him, held his rolled-up catalog to his eye like a spyglass, and said loudly, but to himself, "To see the painting in the painting!"

Standing toward the back of the showroom was Wilhelm Freddie, the artist once housed in Vestre Prison for his exhibition of sexually explicit paintings that later hung at the National Gallery of Denmark. The man wasn't admitted to the Danish Academy of Fine Arts, but he was later considered good enough to teach there. Mr. Larsen was cheerful, and even more so when the paintings started selling like hotcakes.

"I'm sorry," he said to an older lady, "but I can't sell the same piece twice." Then he introduced the woman to Ómar, and they arranged to meet at his studio.

The next morning, when Ómar heard the newspaper drop in through the mail slot, he jumped out of bed. Søndergaard's review was better than he'd dared to hope:

> With these works, the young Icelander shows without a doubt that he has perfect control of technique. It is as if he is playing with a rainbow, so masterly is his control of color. Ragnarsson shows us painting in a slightly different light. . . . This is an exhibit that no true art lover should miss.

The exhibit was popular, and other critics reviewed it favorably. The Icelandic artist had arrived. His work was controversial, he was knee-deep in money, and he relished basking in fame and fortune. Few things, however, irritated him more than Gitte's attempts to enjoy his success with him. He found her intrusive and felt numb when she showed up. What used to give them pleasure and unite them now began to tear them apart.

Gitte constantly nagged him to paint her portrait, waving a photo of herself as a young girl glowing with beauty—the youth she'd repeatedly tried to recapture by going on strict diets, using the right face creams, eating the right foods, and exercising.

She was asking for a portrait not of the person she'd become but, rather, of the one she longed to be. As she sat for the portrait, Ómar began seeing her in a new light.

When Gitte sensed Ómar's diminishing interest, she started feeling jealous. She frequently searched his pockets for something that would give her a clue to his movements during the day. Each time he came home, he was given the third degree. When he tried to leave her, she fell apart and was inconsolable until he promised to stay. The atmosphere in the house was oppressive. Ómar began disappearing alone into the night, frequenting art bars and inviting young women to his studio, where they stayed until the morning hours. He relished coming home smelling of other women only to torture Gitte. He cherished her desperation to believe his lies, even though she knew better. Having this power over her gave him great pleasure. When she begged him to forgive her for something she hadn't done, he didn't forgive her.

Eventually he grew tired of living this double life and told her straight out that it was over between them. When she started sobbing, he kicked her out of the studio, yelling, "You're in my way. Can't you understand we have nothing in common? I'm on an entirely different path from you."

5

AFTER HIS SEPARATION FROM GITTE, Ómar was like a new man, painting with more energy than ever and thoroughly enjoying his sweet life. One day he went to see Mr. Larsen and asked to exhibit his works at Gallery Z, as they had discussed. Mr. Larsen said he was sorry, but the gallery was fully booked for the next two years, and then he wished Ómar all the best.

Next, Ómar went to Gallery Chaos, where the director declined to exhibit his works. He did, however, offer to take some of Ómar's paintings on commission, after reading a review of the Spanish Embassy show. Ómar went to see him every month but always received the same reply: "Don't be so pessimistic, my friend; paintings just don't sell at this time of year."

Ómar wasn't pessimistic. He had learned to hold his head high and knew the importance of being seen at the right places, the ones frequented by the wealthiest art collectors. But when his temporary lack of income had stretched more than six months, his thoughts turned more and more to Gitte.

One evening, when being broke had become unbearable, he called her and asked if she would like to buy a painting. Gitte was delighted to hear his voice and was open to the suggestion. She asked him to come over the following night.

6

FILLED WITH ANTICIPATION, Ómar waited for Gitte's reaction as she regarded the paintings. After a long while, she asked distractedly, "Are you broke, dear?"

"No," he replied. "Things are just tight at the moment . . . but it will be all right."

"You know, these paintings don't appeal to me," she said, looking deep into his eyes.

Ómar found it hard to conceal his disappointment, and to avoid her gaze, he turned away.

"But I can help you," she said tenderly.

"I'll pay you back as soon as I can," he replied, full of gratitude.

"That won't be necessary," she said, taking his hand lovingly and pulling him out of the living room and down a long hallway before stopping at a double door. She opened it and invited him in. In the large room he saw all of his works from the Spanish Embassy show.

"You can keep it all. Maybe you can get a good price for it."

Ómar stood paralyzed and felt the lump settling back into its place in his heart.

"Buying these works was costly," Gitte said warmly, "but the criticism was even more so."

Translated by Sola Bjarnadóttir O'Connell

Killer Whale

ÓLAFUR GUNNARSSON

IT WAS SATURDAY AND OLAF WAS LATE. He had decided to be on time so that his ex-wife wouldn't scream at him, but he was late anyway. They had been divorced for three years now. He spent time with his daughter every Saturday, and for the past six months his ex-wife had had a new husband, with whom she and their daughter lived in a big house right downtown. Once, when Olaf had forgotten to pick up the child, the ex-wife phoned him later that day from the public library, which didn't prevent her from screaming at the top of her lungs—she was a woman born with the heart of a wolf.

The traffic came to a halt, and Olaf looked at his watch and worried. If the early Saturday traffic jam did not dissolve soon, he risked being quite late. He was not good at making plans, or so his ex-wife had always told him. When they had been married, she used to write everything down on bits of paper for him: where to go to find the particular vegetables she wanted, which dry cleaner to use, where to shop and in what order. She would even remind him to go to the post office and check for mail. She numbered all of the places so he would save gas and not spend his time driving from one end of town to the other.

The traffic suddenly began to inch forward, but just when he thought he might slip across the intersection, the light changed to yellow and then to red again, and he was stuck there once more. It was raining a little, and he turned on the windshield wipers as his cell phone rang. It was she, and she was upset, though not quite at the point of yelling.

"You should have been here by now," she said. "Katharine is excited, and she misses you. And she's afraid you might not come!"

"I'm just stuck in heavy traffic," he said. "Bad luck."

"Bad luck, my ass! The traffic is always heavy on Saturday at this time. You know that very well; you should have taken that into account."

"I'm sorry," he said.

"You are insulting your daughter."

She was beginning to raise her voice. He knew that if he objected, she would begin screaming. It was their daughter's illness that had slowly destroyed their marriage.

"Learn to plan things," she said sharply. "That's what I was always trying to teach you."

He thought of saying "I'm a slow learner" but managed to restrain himself, since that would only provide an opening for an argument, and, besides, just at that very moment the light switched to green again and the traffic began to move.

"I'm on my way," he said, trying to add a friendly tone to his voice. "The jam is loosening up," he lied, but by some miracle it turned out to be the truth. A road to the left was just being opened up by city road workers dressed in their fluorescent uniforms, and a whole group of cars went that way, clearing the main road for the remainder of the traffic.

"Well, hurry. You know she's getting very excited, and she can't be allowed to get excited! She just can't!"

He lowered his cell phone and accelerated as much as he could, but, regardless, he could see by the clock in the church tower, which hovered over the city, that he was already ten minutes late.

She lived in an old, sturdy timber house with small windows right down by the city pond in the expensive part of town, and when he finally saw the house in full view, he knew he was far later than he should have been. An ambulance was sitting outside the house, with two wheels up on the sidewalk. He parked his car across the street, and his ex-wife came running down the wooden steps as soon as she saw him.

"Are you insane?" she screamed. "I told you to be on time! You know how much she loves you! She can't tolerate the insecurity of waiting. She's had another attack. And it's a bad one! It's very bad this time! The nurse is with her now. You're lucky she didn't die."

He found himself wondering about that as he hurried up the stairs and entered the house. His ex-wife's new husband, an exceptionally good-looking man who lifted weights and had thick, wavy hair, sat at the table in the parlor wearing an expression of doom. He was a lawyer, and he owned the house. Olaf suddenly felt sorry for the guy. He seemed to know his place already.

Olaf hurried up the next flight of stairs to the nursery. His daughter was in bed, and a young nurse he hadn't seen before was attending to her. The room was spacious, and the pond could be seen through a series of rowan trees. He asked the nurse how the girl was doing.

"She's not feeling very well," the nurse replied. "There is a lot of pus in her lungs, and I've been helping her cough it up."

The nurse rolled the girl back and forth in the bed and lightly hammered on her back. The girl had a blue shade on her usually pink cheeks. "And she lets me know it," the nurse continued. "I know when she lifts her legs that she's angry with me. And she's really angry now. Please come closer so she can see you."

Olaf did as he was told and looked into his daughter's eyes. It was as if they were made of silicone; he saw no sign of recognition.

"I have to remove your mask for a moment," the nurse said to Katharine. "Get ready for it."

She removed the oxygen mask. The girl let out a gasp as the nurse rolled her on her side, and a yellowish froth covered her lips. It seemed to Olaf that Katharine was without the oxygen mask for an eternity, which made him think not of heaven but of hell. His daughter was in hell. This is what hell must be. The nurse put the mask back over his daughter's face, adjusted her limbs here and there, and said, "She's feeling much better. Surprisingly better, as a matter of fact. Were you very close once?"

"We still are," he said.

"I'm so sorry," the nurse said. "A slip of the tongue on my part. I'm truly sorry."

The nurse became hot in the face, and when she blew her hair away from her cheek, he noticed how pretty she was. His ex-wife suddenly appeared in the doorway, and the nurse turned toward her and then slowly shook her head from side to side. The ex-wife disappeared. It made Olaf happy that someone had such power over his ex-wife.

"It seems that your arrival might be the reason why she suddenly feels so much better," the nurse said. This was almost like some sort of flattery, and it made him feel awkward. He looked around the room; it was filled with toys his daughter had once been able to play with. A light brown rocking horse on iron springs with a white mane especially caught his attention. He had bought it for her as a Christmas gift five years earlier, almost at the onset of her illness.

"Will you take her to the hospital?" he asked the nurse.

"No, not this time. Her recovery at the sight of you, as I said, was quite remarkable."

"Tomorrow is Sunday," he said to his daughter. "I'll come for you then if your mama says it's okay. I'll talk to her now. She'll come upstairs right after I leave and tell you if it's okay." He suddenly pulled himself together when he felt the nurse staring at him. "I'll come tomorrow regardless! We can't let another week go by."

The girl looked up at him with such loneliness in her otherwise neutral eyes that he felt himself almost on the verge of asking the pretty young lady standing beside him if she would be willing to go to bed with him. It was an insane thought. He went to the bedroom door and called down to his ex-wife.

"Will you please come look after her now!"

Olaf left the house in the company of the nurse. It was almost as if she protected him from his ex-wife when they met her on their way downstairs.

"Are there many children in the country with this illness?" he found himself asking, knowing full well the answer, but he couldn't think of anything else to say.

"I think there are about three," she replied.

When they arrived at the bottom of the stairs, he said to the husband, who was still sitting at the same place at the parlor table with the same doomed expression, "Would you kindly tell Gudrun I'll be back for the girl tomorrow?"

The man nodded with an expression that seemed to say he wished they would all simply vanish. He didn't even rise to accompany them to the door.

The day outside seemed extraordinarily fresh after such a short visit.

"How long do you expect her to live?" Olaf asked as they walked down the outside steps. The ambulance driver was sitting at the wheel, speaking into a cell phone about something or other, which, judging by the look on his face, was of great importance. When he saw the nurse, he gestured for her to hurry. Olaf already knew the answer to his question, and the nurse confirmed it. "She should be dead by now. Children who start to age prematurely in this manner don't usually live this long."

He felt a strong urge again to ask her to sleep with him, but, given the occasion, this feeling was more than shameful. She was about to get into the ambulance when he was inspired by an idea.

"I'm taking my daughter whale watching tomorrow," he said. "Would you perhaps like to accompany us, if you're available? Or maybe you don't work Sundays? But it would give me a great feeling of security, in case she has some kind of attack." He blushed, adding, "And I'll pay you, of course."

"I would be absolutely delighted," the nurse said. "And you don't have to give me anything. Do you have a piece of paper and a pen so I can give you my phone number?"

He took out his cell phone. "Go ahead, just tell me." He punched in the digits as she told him her number.

He turned around and sent his ex-wife a knowing smile, goading her, and then the ambulance drove away and he got into his car.

Olaf's car was in fact a van. He had a small furniture business and did most of the upholstering himself. The car was equipped to carry his daughter's wheelchair in the back so that the two of them could enjoy their moments together. And when he looked at the empty compartment, it made him think that he had some shopping to do. He was sure he wouldn't be taking any unnecessary detours as he drove across town this time. His ex-wife had always been on him about that.

He decided that he would go and buy some black velvet. He bought all of his upholstery supplies and fabric from an old importer who ran his business out of his home. The importer was nicknamed the Boxer because of his flattened nose—the result of having been kicked by a horse when he was young—and had sold fabric to Olaf's company ever since it was run by Olaf's father. Olaf parked his van on the street where the Boxer lived and walked the path to his house. Both the sidewalk and the path were strewn with leaves. It was autumn now and getting colder. The tourist season was almost over. He would have to check on the whale-watching tours. His daughter's favorite thing to do was to take a boat out into the bay, where the giant animals could be seen rising from the depths to display their massive backs and spout out of their blowholes. This was the only time he really saw life and joy fully rise in her eyes.

When he came closer to the house, Olaf saw that the Boxer was working. Through the window he could see his bald head and massive shoulders outlined against the darkness of the cellar. The Boxer looked up but did not greet Olaf; it wasn't his custom to greet people from his desk. He had a strict set of rules. Even his sons, who were now middle-aged men and worked for their father, were used to knocking before entering the office. Olaf stepped down toward the door, went into the dark corridor, and knocked.

"Come in," a voice said. Olaf entered the office. "I'm about to close for the day," the Boxer said. "You're late. And don't you know it's Saturday? Why don't you come tomorrow?"

"Because I'm working this weekend," Olaf said. "That's why."

The Boxer looked up, surprised. "Well, that's news to me. And you sound like you're serious about it. I don't remember anyone working weekends in the upholstery business, except for your father."

"Well, I'm a changed man," Olaf said. "Something happened."

The Boxer snorted in contempt. "What is it that you need? As I said, I'm about to close up."

"Black velvet!"

"Black velvet?" the Boxer repeated, staring at him. "Now, what do you want that for? Did someone ask you to upholster a coffin?"

Olaf smiled. "No, nobody asked me for that. They're usually done in red, anyway. An old lady wants to redo her sofa and chairs in black velvet, that's all. Is there anything unusual about that?"

"Yes, in fact, there is. I have some in stock, all right. I've had it in stock for years, because nobody's been buying it. But I can see that times are changing."

"Indeed they are," Olaf said.

The Boxer found the keys to the garage, which he used as his storage room, and they headed in that direction. While the old man was fumbling with the lock, he said, "And how is your daughter?"

"Pretty much the same."

The Boxer didn't reply to that but instead said abruptly, "Do you still do that crazy sport of yours?"

"What? No, no, I stopped doing that a long time ago."

"Well, that's good to hear. It always worried your father. He was afraid that you might drown."

"Well, I didn't."

"How is it down there in the deep?"

"It's another world, actually. You forget all about this one."

The Boxer managed to get the door open, interrupting the conversation. They entered the garage. It was a well-maintained, well-heated place because of the need to preserve all of the different fabrics that were stored there.

"Black velvet," the Boxer muttered. "The world is going crazy."

"I thought you'd be happy to get rid of it."

"Yes, in fact, I am. How much of the stuff do you need?"

"About fifty square meters."

"That's a lot."

"It's coming into fashion," Olaf said. "And I want to store up."

The Boxer rummaged around in the piles until he found the black velvet.

"It's old and it's cheap, and it should be just enough for what you need."

"Well, bill me for it, then," Olaf said.

He carried the fabric down to his van. He was a strong man and could manage the load in only one trip. He phoned the tourist-information center when he got home. Yes, they confirmed, there was a whale-watching tour scheduled for the following day, the last one of the season.

Sunday was bright and sunny even though autumn had fully arrived with clear, brisk air around a faded yellow disk of sun. He phoned the nurse. She told him her address. She seemed to be happy to hear from him. Then he phoned his ex-wife and told her when he would be arriving there: two o'clock sharp. He laid the receiver down before she had time to start an argument.

He picked up the nurse, who when dressed in her regular clothes looked even more beautiful than on the previous day. She lived in the eastern part of town, and they chatted a bit while he drove to the city pond. He felt awkward, even a little bit in love. They arrived in front of his ex-wife's house at two o'clock sharp. He opened the back of the van so that he and the ex-wife's new husband could lift the wheelchair and his daughter inside. The girl had her breathing mask on, but he nevertheless thought he could hear her wheeze in pleasure. He shook the husband's hand. He had never known the fellow to utter a single word. His ex-wife stood there on the veranda looking like a general.

When she saw the nurse, she came down to greet her. "When do you think you'll be back?" She addressed the nurse in order to show her contempt for her ex-husband.

"Around five o'clock," Olaf replied nevertheless. "The folks at the whale-watching place said that the trip takes two hours at least."

The ex-wife gave him a glance and nodded. Her husband was so pleased when they were leaving that he even shook hands with Olaf again. Olaf drove toward the harbor. The weather was becoming even more beautiful. He could see that there was snow on the top of the mountain across the bay and for a moment wanted to draw his daughter's attention to it, but then he decided against it because it would require too much effort. And, besides, the nurse was tending to the child tenderly. He liked her more and more all the time.

There was a shop on the street next to the harbor that sold sporting goods: shotguns and ammunition, swimming trunks, gear for scuba diving, footballs, javelins, discuses, running shoes, and so on. He parked the car outside it and said to the nurse, "I have to jump into the shop for a moment to get some things. It won't take long." The nurse nodded.

He took a look at his daughter, who sat there in her wheelchair like a solemn old woman expressing approval of her well-behaved grandson. He went inside; the owner of the shop, whom Olaf was acquainted with, greeted him with a look of surprise.

"Going swimming?" the owner asked. "It's been a while since I've seen you." The owner leaned forward and peered out the window. "And a lady! Congratulations!"

"No, no, not today," Olaf said. "But the autumn weather is simply wonderful. I've been in touch with the guys, and a group of us are going to go for a swim in the bay sometime next week. So I'm going to need a can of grease and a new rubber cap, a yellow one, for my head—and please be quick about it. My daughter is outside in the van, waiting. And, for your information, the lady is her nurse."

The owner of the shop said quickly, so as not to get into a discussion about Olaf's daughter, "You guys are nuts, all of you! You should have been born seals!" He handed Olaf the rubber cap and Olaf tested it. It was a bit tight, but it would do.

"Sea swimming is one of the healthiest sports you can think of," Olaf said. "It makes a man out of you." He nudged the shoulder of the shop owner.

A gorgeous blond, who was inspecting jogging shoes, looked at the two of them and smiled. The owner added up the two items on the till and put them both into a shopping bag.

"Well, give my best to the guys, and be careful not to go too far out," he said. "Watch out for the killer whales—I'm serious."

"Killer whales never attack people except when they're in a pool," Olaf said patronizingly. "And they're only found further to the east."

"I know," the owner replied. "What's the matter with you? Can't you take a joke anymore?"

"I guess not," Olaf said, smiling slightly. "I'm a bit absent-minded today. Well, I have to hurry."

He hurried back to the car and the girls. His daughter sat there in the wheelchair with a satisfied look. They drove down to the waterfront a short distance away. The whale-watching vessel sat at the pier, clearly marked on its stern for the benefit of the tourists. The van rattled a bit on the docks. A lady in a black uniform was selling tickets next to the ship. Olaf and the nurse got out of the van. Olaf walked to the rear of the van, and he could see the sea black and shimmering with oil beneath the planks. He jumped into the back, untied the wheelchair, and rolled it toward the edge; the nurse took hold of the footrests, and together they lifted the wheelchair down on to the dock. Olaf's daughter looked up at the sun blissfully. Olaf rolled the wheelchair to the side of the vessel and paid the lady in black for the tickets.

"Will you be needing any help?" the lady asked, looking at the girl in the wheelchair.

Olaf looked up at the steep stairway that led from the dock to the deck of the boat. With its thin wooden rails screwed onto a platform as a substitute for actual steps, the stairway wasn't exactly suited to wheelchairs, but Olaf had seen worse.

"No, we'll manage," he said.

He took the handles of the wheelchair and walked backward up toward the deck, with the nurse holding onto the footrests. Once they were onboard, Olaf pushed the wheelchair to the rear of the ship. Since the tourist season was coming to a close, there weren't many other whale watchers onboard. He felt comfortable with the nurse and the child, almost as if they were a family.

"You don't know how often I've prayed," he said suddenly.

"Prayed?" she asked curiously.

"Well, perhaps 'prayed' isn't the right word. 'Hoped for a miracle' is maybe a better way of putting it."

"I understand," she said.

He was going to say that she couldn't possibly understand when the engines of the ship suddenly roared, the stairway was removed from the side of the vessel by the staff, and there was a sudden movement as the ship set out to sea. It was only a few kilometers to the whaling grounds, and Olaf walked to the bow of the ship as the nurse pushed the wheelchair behind him. Other passengers gave them kindhearted looks. The gray, autumnlike expanse of the sea appeared hard as steel. He nodded to an older lady, who said she was from America—Phoenix, Arizona, to be precise. She had long dreamt of visiting Iceland with her husband. She introduced Olaf to the elderly man next to her and then said that it had turned out to be more wonderful than either of them had ever expected, but what they had really come to see was the whales. She had heard that there were plenty of them out in the bay.

"Yes," Olaf said, feeling a strange sort of pride, as if the whales belonged to him. He nodded toward his daughter and said, "My daughter loves them."

The American lady said something that he didn't hear, because at that point he noticed there was moisture in his daughter's eyes from the cold breeze. The nurse hadn't seen it, so he wiped the tears away with the back of his hand. His daughter's eyes had more life in them now. She knew she was going to see the whales. She looked at him with love. The nurse was looking out over the bow, shading her eyes with her hands even though the sun was shining on their backs. They continued on for about twenty minutes. Suddenly there was an announcement from the bridge on the loudspeaker: "Whales ahead!"

The sound of the engine decreased and was eventually cut off; the boat slid near to a field of whales that were spouting and snorting and feeding at the surface, in full accord and friendship with humankind, the onlooker. A whaling ban had now been in effect for a quarter of a century, and when officials thought about lifting it, they realized that the tourist trade had become more important, so they extended the ban.

"They don't kill them anymore," Olaf said to the American lady, who nodded her head in approval.

He turned to his daughter, took her out of the wheelchair, and lifted her up in his arms so she could see. The nurse held on to the oxygen mask. The girl was making delightful sounds of joy. And the herd of whales was snorting and wheezing and blowing so that it all sounded like a symphony. The moment lasted a long time, and then the engines started up again and the boat drove in a circle, as if the whales were inside an arena.

When that part was over, the engine came alive again at full power; it was time to head home. Olaf put his daughter back into the wheelchair. She was in a state of total bliss. It made the nurse laugh.

"I think maybe we saw something of the miracle you wished for today," she said.

Olaf smiled slightly but said nothing. For some reason the trip back to the harbor seemed quicker than the trip out. "There weren't any killer whales," the American lady said. "That was a bit of a letdown."

"No, they're loners," Olaf said. "They live in their own herds, by themselves. They don't mix with other whales. They attack them. They feed on them. They're fierce and independent and have no enemies of any kind in the sea. They live by the shore to the east, about three hours from town, but they don't have any whale watching there."

"Oh," the lady said with an odd look in her eyes, and then they took leave of each other.

Olaf waited until all of the other passengers had left the boat. The procedure of getting the wheelchair down the stairway was much the same but now in reverse. Then they rolled the wheelchair to the van. Olaf drove the nurse home. She said good-bye to his daughter. And then she added, when he didn't say anything as she was leaving, "Will I be hearing from you?" Her face flushed a bit.

"Yes," he said, proud and shy. "Yes, you will, definitely. And thank you for asking. You have no idea how much this means to me, especially today."

She looked at him, surprised, and then her face lit up. "Well, I'm glad to hear it, and I certainly look forward to it." She closed the door, and he watched her firm, beautiful figure as she walked toward the house.

Then he looked at his daughter. She was sleeping now, exhausted. That was to be expected. He didn't drive her home but took the road that led out of town. When he came to the intersection that led either east or west, he took the road east. He drove for three hours straight while dusk slowly grew and the landscape changed; the mountains became higher the further he drove into the countryside, and the cliffs with the many caves up high on their faces turned from brown to black as the sun slowly approached the sea. The sky was getting dark, and clouds darker still were set against it. He saw it then, the hill down by the seaside and the cliff beside it, with space enough for a ship to be hauled up between them, and indeed this was the place, legend had it, where the first settlers had landed their ships more than eleven hundred years earlier. The sand on the shore here was as black as a raven for miles around. Olaf drove toward the shore and felt the going becoming heavier when he went off the rough gravel road and on the sand. Then, lying beneath the hill, with the large rock to his left and the waves breaking in front of him, he shut off the engine.

He got out of the car, opened the rear door, and took out the black velvet. He threw the fabric over the car to fully cover it. Then he gathered some stones to hold down the edges, took out a shovel, and piled sand over the edges all around the car. When this was done, he undressed. He had put on his swimming trunks before he left the house in the morning. He took out the jar of grease and covered himself all over. He waited until the very end to cover up the rear of the car. He opened the back door and went inside. His daughter was awake, so he rolled the wheelchair to the edge of the back compartment, lifted it out, and put it onto the sand. Then he took her out of the wheelchair, laid her on the sand, and put the wheelchair back into the car. He considered undressing her and covering her with grease to protect her from the cold, but then thought better of it. It was not the thought of her red, bloated body that made him change his mind, but mercy. The cold would kill her almost instantly. He took the yellow rubber cap he had bought by the store near the harbor, though, and put it on her head. He took out his old black cap and put it on. Then he covered up the edges of the car at the back so that no wind could get under the sand and tear the fabric off. When winter set in, it would be days, even weeks, before the car was found.

Then he lifted the girl into his arms. There was no expression in her eyes. He kissed her on the forehead. He walked into the breakers and began to swim out to sea with his daughter in his arms. The sun was now a glowing disk of fire on the horizon, and flames were jumping out of the sea like molten lead. His daughter's body gave a jolt when it hit the cold water. Then it felt as if she shriveled and got smaller.

He was a good swimmer, used to the sea, and he swam as it slowly got darker and then became pitch black. He knew that she must have been dead from the cold for a long time now. He swam as far out as he could manage, but he was feeling very tired in the legs now, and the cold had started getting to him through the grease coating.

And then the miracle happened. A killer whale surfaced right in front of him. He could see the white patch next to the eye and then the great fin, even though the moon had not come out. The timing on the part of the whale could not have been better, because his strength had given up by then. He embraced his daughter, and they went down into the darkness and the deep.

Translated by Stephen Meyers and Ólafur Gunnarsson

The Secret Raven
Service and Three Hens

ÞÓRUNN ERLU-VALDIMARSDÓTTIR

Prologue

TWO RAVENS SIT ON ODIN'S SHOULDERS *and speak into his ear all the tidings that they see or hear; they are called thus: Huginn (thought) and Muninn (memory). He sends them at daybreak to fly about the entire world, and they come back at undern-meal; thus, he is acquainted with many tidings. Therefore, people call him Raven-God.*

The three most important norns, Urðr (Fate, Wyrd), Verðandi (Present), and Skuld (Future), come out from a hall standing at the Well of Urðr (Well of Fate), and they draw water from the well, and with it the clay that lies around it, and sprinkle it over the Ash Yggdrasill so that its limbs shall not wither or rot.

....

Three years ago, two ravens got burned onto the floppy drive in my head. My mom wanted me to walk my brother home after school. That day I was like an idiot at the front door; when I was about to open it, I didn't have the key in my pocket, not wearing the same coat as usual and no key. I thought of trying to get Nonni through the window if it was open. It's easy to climb to the lower roof. We climbed on the top of a barrel, and from that I lifted Nonni up to the roof and crawled up behind him, but the window was latched too hard. I tried to loosen the latch with a pen but couldn't, and so there was nothing to do but sit down and call Mom.

She said she'd come as soon as she could, so we just sat there. I had some leftover lunch, a cold hot sandwich with ham, cheese, and pineapple that Mom used to always make back then. We took turns taking bites and Nonni got the hiccups and we laughed and this wasn't so bad, sort of nice to see the world from a different angle, from above, like birds. Dusk was falling slowly and serenely like a big black hat. But then smack into giggles and well-being, a disgusting crowing cut through so close that it turned my blood to ice. I barely dared to ease over to the roof edge and then saw it in the garden below: two ravens hovering over some delicacy.

"Nonni, don't look! Bloody hell, they're eating something! They're eating a cat!" I yelled at Nonni, and the ravens got so startled that they fluttered upward, but settled down again. Oh, my God, what were they doing!

"Don't look!" I said when I sensed Nonni by my side. This was too horrible for me, let alone poor little him, I thought. Nonni moved as close as he could, excited and delighted to watch this real-life horror movie. We clearly saw the ravens pick at the cat with their sharp beaks so tufts of hair went flying. Luckily the blood didn't seem to splash—and it was getting dark.

"What kind of cat is this?" asked my brother. "It's a lot bigger than Skotta."

I squint my peepers and try to glean through the darkness which cat this is and think it's old Brandur from next door, and suddenly I get furious, like the lioness inside me suddenly awakes. I jump down from the roof onto the barrel like a hero in an animated movie. I grab an old shovel by the house and attack the ravens with all the nastiest words I know. Fuck! Damn you bastards, go away bloody bastards! I forget to be afraid.

I scare the predators off and kneel down next to the poor kitty, touch his paw, and it is cold, sort of frozen. I tell my brother that the kitty was already a corpse when he became dinner. Our eyes adjust to the darkness down in the garden. The ravens started on the shiny stuff—drawn to glitter like glam rockers. The eyes were gone, just dark holes now. Ravens have beaks specially designed to pick out eyes and are quick to do so. They were well into eating the insides of Mr. Brandur, the most stylish cat in the west part of town; the stomach was open, and guts and long intestines are outside. Yuck!

We hear them crowing and see them sitting above us, these guys, mildly annoyed, raven black and horribly cruel and nonchalant, like they have been ousted away from a normal dinner. They sit with mussed heads and blood on their beaks on the white castle house on the next street. Ominous, and not just a little . . . the hungry raven eyes are like spears in my back.

We sit still even though the cold is gnawing at us. Nonni says the ravens need to eat. "It's allowed to give them leftovers," I say, and I sense that I'm sounding like Grandpa. But we can't go inside to get a plastic bag or anything, because Mama is nowhere in sight. But then a light comes on on the middle floor in the house where Brandur lives. I know it's cruel to send Nonni to let the woman know, but there's no other way. . . . I sit still, angrily clutching the shovel.

He was buried in the backyard. Mama called to us through the open kitchen window. We watched the woman half sobbing, holding a Ten-Eleven bag while her husband dug a hole in the frozen earth. The scratching, like nails on blackboard. Your time is up, kitty, and the worms will get the rest.

You can understand that after this, I started to think of ravens as disgusting creatures. I felt a stab of fear when I heard crowing and saw the ravens huddle on the roof of Landakot Hospital, smelling people in the death wards. The raven was here to stay on my sense-planet—my ears started to perk up like those of a terrified field mouse every time I heard it. To rid myself of fear,

I started reading everything I could find about ravens, hoping I would stop being such a baby and a scared simian with a shovel, and become a female version of "the sane man" in ninth grade. Mama says that those who can't stand horror need to learn how to inure themselves. I ordered a tape and a book on the Internet, from amazon.co.uk.

It is possible to teach tame ravens words in human-speak, and people can learn raven words. Ravens predict what will be, but foremost they predict death, because they see infrared color around sick animals before they die. That is why they perched on top of churches in the olden days and stared at people who were marked for death. They wanted meat. They see in animals like us these weird colored auras that we can't see ourselves, which occur when we're heading toward some demise. Then they fly toward us, because they can see in us the colors of angst that might turn us into carcasses. When we glow in colors of health and good fortune, they fly over us from behind and have no interest in such specimens of upright mammals in clothes. That is why old beliefs say it's a sign of prosperity if a raven flies along with you.

Ravens were used for hunting in the olden days, before hawks and falcons. In the Middle Ages, ravens never missed a battle site. The raven appeared as soon as soldiers donned their fighting gear and followed them to battle, because it knew to expect good human meat! Back then it was the norm to leave the enemy army lying on the ground for dogs and ravens— battles ended in a feast for them.

I owned the book *Gods and Heroes* from Norse literature, unread, but after the ravens ate Brandur, I found a sudden need to read it. Ravens are emblems of the head god, Odin. I started feeling like I had been randomly selected, because how many girls get to see a raven eat a cat? Except that in mythology there is no random—all continuance is woven by the norns of fate, who show up when we are born to create our future. Odin, the raven-god, had the raven's intuition to rule over the battlefield and be wise like the raven, the sagest of birds. He lost one eye, just like a raven victim, but without his help. Odin sold his eye for a sip from the well of wisdom and became so wise that he understood ravenspeak. The ravens on Odin's shoulders are named Huginn and Muninn. When they fly over the world and search for tidbits, it's Odin himself traveling in the shape of a bird. Whatever the raven gleans, the god will soon know. They fly over the entire world daily and crow in his ear everything they see and hear. He is fluent in ravenspeak! He is one with them.

Upon my raven musings, I learned to read the raven's death prediction, but I didn't suspect that prediction magic was still fully valid. I thought science had driven all such nonsense out of the world. What happened that summer was a total time shift, as if it had happened a gazillion years ago, when the ravens were still conducting their daily flight—so low, fluttering the hair of the three norns by the roots of the tree of life, Yggdrasil. . . .

Mama and her friends were going crazy, because the summer was ending and they just had to get to a country cottage. They are all professional nutjobs—artists. After oohing and aahing over the beauty of the countryside, the clouds, the lava, and the mountains along the way, we finally came down to where the vista of the south coast spread before us and pulled up to a farmstead and a cottage next to a small old church. The luggage was brought in, and food and drink, and Mama like a robot immediately made the beds and set our phones to charge. Then there were drinks, and they smoked out on the patio, so jolly that I just had to laugh at them, and they smiled back and thought I was laughing with them.

The weather is so nice that we're all wearing light clothes. We carry just a gift in a bag and a key in the pocket. We're heading over to the farmhouse to thank their friend for the cottage. The thanks are sloshing around—in the form of a large whiskey bottle. Magnus is not a farmer but rather someone they kiss up to, a recent emigrant from downtown Reykjavík, where Mama's friends live.

Nonni and I lag behind, out of reach with our regular world but not annoyed. The weather is excellent, shiny like the high they're on, and it's infectious. Here, at least, are horses and everything screaming green. The light is so bright you can see spiders up in the mountain. An ugly woolly cloud passes over the mountain. We walk across the moor, which is decorated with daisies and names of other flowers that have been stuffed down my throat for years. Now it's daisy time; the dandelion and buttercup season is over. Mama, Eva, and Ragnhildur are at the height of silliness. The innocent-looking church inches closer, all set to tease us.

The dog comes running and acts friendly, but there's still a dark look in his eyes, so I'm careful. He bends down, so I crawl to show him submission. He is nice . . . nice right back, but I sense there is something wrong. He rolls onto his back with his feet in the air, surrendering, and I do the same. Then he seems to smile with his eyes. He sees that I'm OK.

After seeing such a sad dog, I'm not surprised to see no joy in the wife. She seems irritated that these bitches should show up with whiskey for her husband. They're not at all interested in her, just plop down in the kitchen happy as can be, already in the forest of Bacchus, as my grandpa would say. The wife is heading to the freezing point. The three of them think Magnus is awesome, fluff themselves up, and stick out their breasts. There's just something about the guy, even I can feel it. Not just fame or self-confidence, just something that is nice to be near.

He chats and is upbeat. They continue sipping the whiskey, except the wife has a lot of lines on her upper lip and sips coffee alone in a corner. He says he'll get three hens tomorrow. Mama's friend Ragnhildur has become so cheerful that she says, "You should name them after us, Thora, Eva, and Ragnhildur!" She smiles with shiny eyes, rocks inside herself, and raises her glass. Magnus looks at this wife and says, "Nooo."

I choke on my soft drink, because I see she's standing up stiffly. Mama sees like I do that the wife doesn't want to feed hens for the next decade that are named after some bitches from the city who come to get her husband drunk and preen like geese in front of him. . . . Mama tries to save the day.

"Just call them Urdur, Verdandi, and Skuld." She looks at me and gets a grin in return. Magnus wipes his mouth with the back of his hand, thinks about it, and sticks his tongue deep into the whiskey, and I feel admiration for him when he says, "Urdur, Verdandi, og Skuld."

He is totally OK. They laugh loudly, almost foaming, but the wife leaves and slams the door behind her. I feel eerie. I am raven-crazy enough to sense a cold vibe go through the house and through me. The norns have arrived.

When they deem themselves drunk enough, he wants to show us the church, and Nonni and I tag along. We walk directly across the rocky moor, and the dog starts panting, obviously old. He also has some bald spots and wear in his fur. He pants but follows anyway, raven black in the sunshine, while the church gets a little closer. The hairs on my own little head fur stand up, because I hear what I didn't need to hear, crowing, very close by. A raven flutters just above us, close enough so that I can count his feathers. He sees we're heading toward the church, flies around the little steeple, and alights on the top of the cross. Sitting still with his heavy eyes trained on us, I feel like he's looking through me, at the dog, at Magnus. Or was he looking at Mama or Eva? He scrutinizes us all. I know he's reading our auras, and since he's paying so much attention to us going to church, someone, according to old legends, is doomed. It's as though he can see carcasses-to-be, shells-to-be. It is like Magnus can hear my thoughts, because he says, "Someone will die," then adds a deep ha ha ha.

There is no wall around the church, just a concrete gate with an arc and a cross. Just a gate but no wall. Everything open. We hear the horse neigh before it comes around the corner of the church, shaking his bowed head with each step. He is . . . yes . . . he is black. Three black creatures; this is a triple. Help! I try to push my thoughts away by poking Nonni. This is starting to look like an unreal play.

We enter the church, and Magnus pulls the door shut behind us. It's as if it's too big, but he is strong and cool and yanks until it clicks into its groove. They walk down the aisle, and I see my brother out of the corner of my eye fiddling with the old-fashioned key. They are acting very unchurchlike, giggling and squealing. Lots of "gees" and "goshes," the bottle and constant flirting moving back and forth, they might as well break into dance—all the swaying and posing is graceful enough. My brother and I sit in pews across the aisle and look at each other silently. We don't need to articulate anything, we are thinking the same thing—damn, they look idiotic. Finally Magnus makes his way to the doors to let the superwomen Urdur, Verdandi, and Skuld out, but the doors refuse to open. He is big and attacks the doors, jiggling the keys, cursing, and mutters, "I don't get it," and Mama says something like, "God, is it locked?" They suddenly become dead serious, we are locked in a church and the windows can't be opened. Sleep here? No one has a cell phone. Claustrophobia crawls up the walls like moss at the speed of a mouse.

Finally they get so serious that it's like it has dawned on them they're misbehaving in a house of God. They walk up to the altar, crossing themselves and thinking, "You great eternal higher power, forgive us for coming here and acting like fools." They're seriously rattled, reacting in a whiskey haze but more afraid than we are.

This impromptu holy moment appears to drive out the demon in them. Magnus suddenly takes on a minister's demeanor, and the ladies act like the members of a choir. He looks at us with these new cantor eyes, makes the sign of the cross toward the altarpiece, which depicts Jesus on a cloud on a black background, and walks all worshipful up the aisle. He pauses before he turns the old key, but now calmly, with a secure grip, and . . . the doors open, thank

God! Much relief and sighs. Ah, nice fresh air and daylight. Mama, who is always trying to wash my mouth out with soap, says, after our good-byes and while we are striding back to the cottage, "That was really creepy."

But it isn't over yet. In the car on the way home the next day, Mama and her friends are a sorry sight, the joy bank in their brains isn't yielding any interest, the whiskey has depleted their funds. Music on the radio might help, but we hear only the daily death announcements, and the raven in me is screaming, and I think—someone died. Then the droning voice mentions the farmer my mother stayed with when she was a child. He died at his home yesterday. I can feel everyone in the car stiffen except my little brother, who is blissfully ignorant.

How could the raven know that someone Mama knows was dying? Was this decided a long time ago, or do time and space not exist? Norns, tall and slender with birdlike heads, flutter across the screen on my chest.

Mama is so polite that she calls Magnus that evening and thanks him for lending us the cottage. That is when he tells her the dog died. He had a stroke. I am rather relieved to hear this, because now I can believe in science again: the raven on the steeple saw just the red aura of a sick dog. The horse was just a coincidence, just sensitive to something funny in the air or just wanted to eat some of the juicy grass on the graves. Everything is normal and scientific, no magic except in the realm of the impossible. I am again just something that swam the fastest out of Daddy . . . no norns hovering over my newborn self deciding on the course of my life.

In a silly fit I go biking with Nonni, because we were a bit subdued after sitting in a car with the solemn women. It isn't just the liquor but also that God locked them in a church after a raven predicted a death that affected them. They are better solemn, sort of.

We bicycle by the shore. I bike way too fast, and the path is wet, and Nonni, who is a lazy and inexperienced biker but wants to ride as quickly as I do, goes much faster than he can handle. The asphalt is uneven due to a flood awhile back, his bike skids, and he goes flying and lands right on his head and then lies absolutely still. I don't see him fall, don't hear it either. I am going at full speed, but I look back after a bit. I turn around and pedal back to look for him and finally see him there like a corpse and go mad with fear, kneel down next to him and embrace him and lift him up, cradling him in my arms, but he doesn't move and he's not pretending. He is conked out, but not dead; I can feel he is alive. He is breathing. Then I remember that you should never move people with head injuries and try to lay him gently down again. I am sobbing. I call Mama, crying for help, and after an eternity an ambulance arrives. . . . All I can think about is, Oh, my God, two dead and is Nonni the third?

He came to on the way to the hospital, but didn't know who he was for a few hours. They kept him for a few days. The three black creatures by the church tripled the raven death prediction—but there is still the eeriest of all. Eva's mother also died. She was the third one. She had a stroke the week after that weekend. She was very lucky, said Mama, to live on so that no one found her before she was completely gone. It is not desirable to become a bedridden vegetable in diapers.

But within our little family unit everything is just fine. Not to mention my own notions about life. I now know that it is deep, mysterious, and weird, and full of evil mixed with the good.

All that lives will be consumed or burned. I was forced to that understanding, and since then I think the life inside me is amazing and see how everything on this planet is connected. The raven's beak is specially designed to pluck one of my eyes out! My hand is specially designed to pick fruit at the supermarket. Inside me is a hugely complex program that keeps my life going and saves my little world.

It is still okay to be afraid—it's a natural emotion, just like going mad over how cute a certain boy or a beautiful baby is. I am thinking of being moderately afraid in the hope of then being better equipped to deal with the lions that I know the norns are weaving into my web. No one escapes. It is possible to be mad with joy and beauty anyway.

Translated by Sola Bjarnadóttir O'Connell

One Hundred Fifty Square Meters

KRISTÍN EIRÍKSDÓTTIR

THEY HAD TO TAKE THE APARTMENT. A hundred fifty square meters for KR 100,000 was a ridiculously affordable price. Many of their friends who lived in windowless basement rooms paid a similar amount. The location was also fine—not great, not right downtown, but pretty good. The landlord seemed determined to see them as future tenants. Nothing else seemed possible.

So they said they would move in at the end of the month. At the same time they would lose a thirty-square-meter apartment in Nordumyri that they had rented for KR 130,000 for the past year. The owner's daughter was unexpectedly on her way home from studying abroad, and since Dani and Aesa were subletters, there was nothing they could do. They had two weeks to find something else and empty out the apartment.

"Oh, my God," said their friends Katla and Gummi, "you'll end up in a kid's room with some distant relative. The rental situation is a lot worse since you last looked."

"A year ago?" stammered Aesa, and Katla shook her head.

"Twice as bad, and you can't imagine what's acceptable these days." Then she pulled out her laptop and located an ad on Facebook. "Forty-square-meters windowless cave in upper Breidholt for 170,000. See what I mean?" she asked, and Aesa choked up. Dani was irritated.

"It will work out somehow," he said. "In the worst case, we can pitch a tent in Laugardalur and it will be fine. Aesa and I will just be in a camping mode until everyone else moves to Norway and more apartments become available."

"He doesn't care," said Aesa, and wanted to be shocked but was a little proud of him. He actually didn't care if they had to live on the street.

"He wants us to end up on the streets," she giggled.

"You don't have children," said Katla, who was now visibly irritated. Gummi added that until children made an appearance, reality was of no consequence. That evening when they went to bed, Aesa started getting worried. In her mind, she went over everyone she knew and whether anyone had a summer cottage that wasn't being used, preferably within an hour's driving distance from Reykjavík. She worked at a clothing store on Main Street and had to be able to get to work.

Dani was an artist. Ever since he graduated, he just hadn't found any opportunities. Aesa thought he should have tried harder, but Dani was convinced that the crash had erased his professional field altogether. At the moment, he called his unemployment checks his small artist's grant and relished tending to his art all day long. Once his unemployment payments ended, he'd look for work on a fishing boat. But until then, he preferred not to waste time worrying. In other words, he was at home and didn't care if they ended up in an abandoned ghost house way out in the country. He had, in fact, sometimes mentioned that they should find some abandoned farm and slowly renovate it any way they wanted, and farm the land.

She generally thought it a great idea, for about half a minute, or until she remembered who she was and knew she would die of boredom if she could never see anyone but Dani. She'd waste away from boredom if she had to look at the same moor from morning to night and wait for something green to peek out of the ground.

She would prefer to live on Bank Street and be able to pop home whenever she was out partying and then even pop out again—or hear partying noises when she opted to not go out. Perhaps she would drink less if she could always hear the noise from people. Perhaps she would stop feeling like she was always missing out on something.

The rental was advertised on craigslist. Dani found it and contacted the owner. He said the apartment had been empty for a while, and they could come and take a look whenever they wanted. He lived nearby and could be there on short notice. They went there right away, and the entire time, Aesa kept talking about how awful Reykjavík was east of Snorrabraut.

"Oh, stop it," said Dani, and asserted that the Voga area was an old green neighborhood. "Maybe there's a garden," he added, and Aesa said, "Who wants to slave away in a rented garden?"

"You're so acquisitive," he said seriously, and Aesa said she didn't even know what that meant.

"It means you think only about profit and not real value," he tried to explain, and soon they were in a fight. Aesa got teary at the thought that he'd consider her stingy. Because it was so unfair, but Dani wasn't saying she was stingy. He was saying she was preoccupied with ownership in general, and that was different from being stingy. In the end, he had to repeat a few times that Aesa was the most generous person he knew—which was also true—and then she cheered up again but was no closer to understanding the meaning of the word "acquisitive."

....

The apartment was on the second floor of a two-family house, and behind it was a small unkempt yard, full of weeds, junk, and tall yellow grass. The landlord stood on the steps, a gray old man

wearing shades and a long parka. He was in the middle of a cough-
ing fit when they arrived at the house, but he quickly recovered
and reached out with the hand that had been in front of his mouth
moments earlier.

He introduced himself as Hinrik, and he said the front door
was warped and the lock not working, but promised to have it all
fixed before they moved in.

They entered into a tiled foyer filled with overcoats and a shoe
rack full of footwear. The odor was immediately unpleasant, with
a sour hint of pipe smoking. Aesa wrinkled her nose and peered
into a narrow, dark hallway.

"The furniture is still here," said Hinrik apologetically, and it
would work out best for him if it could stay.

"Is this your furniture?" asked Aesa, but the man said the
owner had left things this way and no one would come to clear it
out.

"Is he dead?" she asked, and he said he simply didn't know. He
had lived there for thirty years and then one day suddenly vanished without a trace. Hinrik was his sister's lawyer, and she had
advertised and posted notices and been very much in the media
fanfare that followed, but then refused to have anything to do with
the practical matters in the case. She had, for instance, never been
to her brother's home to remove his things. All very strange, Hinrik thought.

"And you would think it's best if we live with all his stuff and
don't change anything?" asked Dani.

"Well, you can of course arrange things any way you want, so
to speak. . . . Just don't throw anything out that looks like it has
personal value. The thing is that seven years need to pass after a
disappearance before it's possible to, well . . ."

"And you trust us to evaluate what has worth and what is
trash?"

"Oh, you mean . . ." Hinrik looked flustered.

"What about the small stuff? Like clothes and things?"

"Well, it would be best if you could just put everything in one room. Surely the two of you won't need the whole 150 square meters just for yourselves."

The living room was painted brown. The sofas were made of thick, quiltlike leather patches, and every possible surface was littered with souvenirs, elephants, puppets, and miniature temples and castles.

The kitchen was neat, but on the table was a plate with crumbs and an empty coffee cup.

"How long ago did he disappear?" asked Dani, and the man thought about it for a moment.

"Maybe a year by now," he said. "Yes, a whole year has gone by."

"Is this his?" asked Aesa, pointing at the plate and the cup.

"Well, this . . ." replied the man. "I just didn't have the where-withal to wash it up."

"And you want us to do it?" Dani asked. "Or do you want us to live here with this plate, crumbs, and cup just sitting there?"

The man grimaced. "I know it seems strange," he said, "but it just doesn't pay to keep apartments empty, and I'm not actually allowed to touch anything. His sister agreed to put it on the rental market but didn't want anything else to do with it. We're in a bit of a legal limbo here."

The bedroom was large, with windows facing the yard, and on the double bed were black linens bunched up on a gray fitted sheet. One wall was hidden by a wardrobe, and on another was a faded print of a Gauguin painting. A naked black-haired girl with her back to the viewer held her hair in a ponytail, watching another girl who was kneeling. The walls were painted eggshell blue.

"Let's put his stuff in here," said Dani decisively, and Aesa nodded. She didn't want to sleep in the vanished man's bedroom, and besides, this was the largest room in the apartment next to the living room.

"Yes," said the landlord. "Then there's the study."

Books obscured the study walls. Next to the window was a

large desk covered in papers, with an old-fashioned computer in the middle. Dani examined the book spines while Aesa chatted with Hinrik. There were no novels among the books, just journals and mostly books about politics, interviews, and memoirs of world leaders. Most of them were about the Cold War.

"What did he do?" asked Aesa ". . . Or does he do?"

"He's a political scientist," replied Hinrik, "but I don't know if he worked as one . . . or whether he was a part-time lecturer at the University of Iceland. I seem to remember something about that."

"Didn't he have children?"

"No, he was, to tell you the truth, sort of special. His sister said she didn't think he ever had romantic relationships."

"Do you have a picture of him?"

Hinrik opened a filing cabinet and pulled out a clear folder with some photos. Aesa leafed through it and mentioned they all seemed a bit dated. One picture was of a twenty-year-old college graduate, the others even older—a small boy on a rocking horse or playing with a toy truck. He was always alone in the photos.

"He's so cute," said Aesa, smiling, and Dani said the books were pretty much all from before the fall of the Berlin Wall.

"He was very preoccupied with the Cold War," said Hinrik absentmindedly, "and nuclear weapons. He mentioned atomic bombs every time we met, I think."

"So, you did know him?"

"Yes, not well, but I helped the siblings with their mother's estate a few years ago."

....

"You do realize that this will be like living with the guy," said Aesa on the bus ride home.

"Yeah . . ." said Dani and fell silent for a while. "Still, 150 square meters for 100,000 is a steal."

"There's so much work to do. For example, I cannot live in a poop-colored living room, and once we fill the rooms with his stuff, there'll probably only be 80 square meters left. And did you see the bathroom? If there isn't some disgusting mold under the plastic wallpaper, then I don't know what."

"What? Did you notice he never mentioned how long we could stay there? At least six years, Aesa. Imagine, we don't have to deal with the rental market for six years. The old man just wants to get out of dealing with the apartment. Can't you see this is a great opportunity? Besides, I want that study. I can use a lot of the books."

It took them a week to clean the apartment and make it livable. When Aesa mentioned to Hinrik she wanted to paint it, a tortured look came on his face that she immediately interpreted as no.

"What if he comes back?" she asked Dani. "What if Hinrik knows somehow that the man isn't dead at all and that he could reappear at any time? If that's why he doesn't want us to paint and why we can't throw anything out . . ."

"The odds that a man who's been gone for a year will show up are very, very small, Aesa. Really."

"But if he really was so special, that man, maybe he just took off on a trip around the world and forgot to tell anyone."

They moved in at the end of the month. The bedroom was filled to the rafters with souvenirs and junk. In the dining room was a pullout couch they unfolded every night and used for a bed. Their clothes hung on racks on the door that closed to the living room. They had so little furniture after moving between rentals the past few years that they decided to use some of the existing pieces. The brown quilted leather sofas were still there, the TV set, and the Santos Palisander coffee table with a cigarette-burn mark. Everything was clean. Aesa had scrubbed every inch and felt better while doing it, like she was removing dried slime from the house.

She burned incense and tacked Dani's drawings on the walls. She rang bells and sprinkled water in every corner.

"Come those who wish to come, and leave those who wish to leave, stay those who wish to stay, and not harm me and mine," she muttered.

Dani usually got up around noon, made himself some coffee, and settled into his new study, which had, to him, a sort of eerie attraction. He rifled through the vanished man's personal papers, read his books, and went through his computer files. He examined every detail carefully and with each passing day got a more complete picture in his head. At first, he was convinced the man was afflicted with some sort of paranoia or psychosis. He found diaries in which all the entries were about U.S. military spying in Iceland, but once he read through them, what stayed with him was a cool, logical tone that in no way indicated a man deep in psychosis.

Sometimes he went to a coffeehouse or to the bar with his friends, but he liked staying home in the study best, drinking beer and reading or drafting possible versions of his project: the Cold War in the vanished man's head. He took some books and cut out sentences that he then glued on paper. He tore pages from the man's diaries, used them as a base, and made collages that looked like blown-up details from one of the man's childhood photos. Aesa came home late in the evenings, usually too drunk to have conversations with, and was gone before Dani woke up.

Luckily she didn't have to stay at home all day like Dani. Actually, it happened that more often she had a bite downtown with her friends and went to a bar. Then she came home on the last bus or walked if she missed it. On regular weekdays, she had to get up early to go to work, and every other weekend she worked at a nursing home. The truth was that she felt terrible in the new rental. She felt like there were three of them living there: she, the invisible Cold War enthusiast, and Dani, who talked of nothing else.

What she had experienced before as a revolutionary—or even anarchistic—view of life was starting to sound more and more like something out of a book. Dani studied speeches that were all based on black-and-white thinking that divided people into two groups: evil people and virtuous people. These speeches sounded familiar and reminded her of the arguments at childhood family dinners.

Her grandfather usually counted himself as one of the good guys and accused her father, the MBA, of being a selfish capitalist parasite.

Everyone was selfish, especially Aesa, whom the grandfather judged to be afflicted with the notion that she could have everything for nothing. When he was young and fought along with the unions to improve the workers' standard of living, he had never imagined the results would entail this lazy, idling youth who overturned the financial system by becoming bankrupt before the age of thirty and then stuffed herself with gold flakes to celebrate.

"It isn't this simple, Dani," she said once when Dani had been going on and on about the brainwashing of the American people. The brainwashing consisted of making the victim believe he had a choice, but later stripping him of everything and thereby blaming all shortages on him.

"Not this simple?" Dani said, lighting the pipe he had found in the vanished man's drawer and recently started smoking—to save money. "Please explain to me how this is more complicated."

"I mean, it's got to be possible to think about it another way," said Aesa. "The world is not *The Lord of the Rings*. These aren't just Communist hobbits versus capitalist Sauron. . . ."

"What is the American empire other than Sauron?" asked Dani happily. "Excellent comparison, by the way. . . ."

Perhaps what irritated her most were the subtle changes. The braggart tone in his voice was even worse than his assertions, and it was like he smelled different. Pipe-tobacco odor was one thing, but there seemed to be the added scent of old age. She couldn't think of a different description when she tried to explain this to her girlfriend.

She tried talking to him one morning when, against all odds, he got up at the same time she did. That was because she noticed that things they had stuffed into the bedroom had migrated into the rest of the apartment. The carving of an African woman with a tub on her head was hanging over the phone table, and the Gauguin print was on the wall in the room where they slept.

Dani just laughed at her and said he was going to use these things in an installation about the Cuban Revolution.

"Why don't you do a piece on the Arab Spring instead?" she asked, but Dani pretended like he didn't hear her and broke into a speech about Che Guevara and Kennedy. While he rambled on, he stuffed the pipe, and to Aesa he suddenly seemed hunched over or somehow smaller.

....

One day, about six months after they moved in, Dani realized that he had barely looked at his girlfriend for days. His project consumed him, as had happened so many times before, but then she usually made sure the connection between them didn't break. This time, it was as if she had given up. The few times they had coffee together and lay side by side in bed, she was quiet and distant. Their communications were friendly but superficial, and he had been too busy to notice.

He called her at work and asked if she would be home for dinner. She said she had decided to see her friends, but Dani promised to cook. She reluctantly agreed to break her date and head straight home. Dani went to the store and bought a filet of haddock and potatoes. Then he went to the liquor store for a magnum of white wine. He spent the remainder of the afternoon cleaning and cooking. When Aesa came home, he had lit candles and the haddock was in the frying pan, the wine in a carafe. Aesa smiled hesitantly in the doorway.

"How nice," she said. "What is that sweater you're wearing?" Dani had felt a bit chilled and put on a sweater that was on the chair in the study. A patterned machine-knit sweater with holes in the elbows.

"Is that the man's sweater?" she asked, and Dani looked down at it.

"Well . . ." he replied, and felt a sudden sharp pang of shame, he didn't know from where.

"I will not talk to you in his clothes."

Dani took the sweater off and tossed it in the trash.

"I can't talk to you while I know that sweater is in the trash," said Aesa, and Dani took the trash outside. When he returned, Aesa was sitting at the kitchen table, still wearing her coat.

"I can't live here," she said. "The Cold War is over. I mean, I might as well move in with my grandfather than live with you."

"When is a war over?" asked Dani. "When the last scarred person dies? What about the invisible scars?"

"I'm moving out tonight," said Aesa, staring at Dani's face. He looked away, put food on his plate, sat up straight, and started eating.

She packed only the bare necessities. Dani had heard her talking on the phone with her friend, and shortly thereafter he heard a car parking outside. He finished the food on his plate, then poured himself some wine and called out to her.

"What?" she said from the doorway, and he thought she looked like she had cried a little bit.

"You can expect destruction from the sky, the likes of which have never been seen before on earth," he whispered.

Translated by Sola Bjarnadóttir O'Connell

Grass

ANDRI SNÆR MAGNASON

IT'S AMAZING THAT PEOPLE THINK the guy who mows their lawn in the summer has no other interests besides grass. After four years at this summer job, I've become quite an expert in conversing about grass. I can keep up a conversation with the grass owner for hours on end and talk about only grass, even though I'm bored to death with it. But what wouldn't I do when paid by the hour? Grass shouldn't have yellow roots, I tell them, because that means it's overgrown. Too much fertilizer damages grass, and it cannot have too much moss or dandelion either, although I don't really know why, and you cannot smoke grass (people never get this one). Many are filled with joy if I tell them their lawn was much harder to mow than the one next door. They then think they got more bang for their buck.

Class, social status, or opinions are of no consequence; everyone is equal when conversations include grass, and for that I pay dearly. Even though I'm bored to death, I can hardly quit. This is a well-paying job, and I've already invested in an electric trimmer that mows the lawn ten times as fast as a mechanical scythe.

I could never keep my sanity if I didn't have the poets' group to turn to. We are nine guys who meet regularly in a hundred-year-old house next to the old cemetery on South Street. We drink red wine or brandy, discuss literature, and read from our own works, poetry and stories, translations, and even scientific articles. Sometimes older authors come and present their latest works. We're considered a promising group. Some of us have published books that received positive reviews, including me.

The other day I was mowing the lawn for one of my regulars, full throttle. The strings of the trimmer whirled like invisible chopper blades, cutting gashes into the rows of straw. Strewing them all over the place. Green sap and pieces of grass whirled everywhere and covered my orange overalls, so they looked fuzzy, like a kiwi. Sometimes snails joined in, hitting me in the face. The slime tastes worse than dandelion milk, though the snails themselves are surprisingly easy to get used to and quite soft to bite into.

I thought of the golden plover in a nest that I accidentally mowed down last summer. Blood. Eggshells. Feathers. Sometimes I actually want to work wearing a black sheath, like the man with the scythe himself. Armed with a maniacal grin, I would tranverse the field like a flame. Ha ha. No straw spared. Vroom. Vroom. Swish. Kill. Kill. I would hear the echo of cries of pain and gnashed teeth, pleasantly faint through my ear protectors, as if from the great beyond.

I shut off the machine, and the odor of gasoline mixes with the smell of grass. The lawn owner heads over. He is a trotting wholesaler who adores dead artists. I remove my ear protectors, though I would rather keep them on, and turn the left side of my brain off and get ready to have a grass discussion.

"Hi, Grassman," he says.

"Hi," I say.

A short silence while we both view the results of the day's work.

"That was a rather fine book you gave me the other day," he says.

"Well, did you read it?" I ask, surprised.

"No, my sister read it. I was going to ask you if you could mow her lawn, too."

"I suppose I could. Is she interested in literature?" I ask, hoping to finally come across someone who can talk about things other than grass.

"I guess so. She's a writer."

"Really? What's her name?"

"Her name is Gunnlod, and she lives in Skerjafjordur, 13 Bauganes Street."

Yes, Gunnlod. I knew who she was. She had written a couple of perfectly OK books, and we once considered asking her to a reading. Finally, someone who could talk about something other than grass. Gunnlod had achieved some success, and if someone had to name a female author, she was usually mentioned first.

The next day I get into my car, a red Peugeot 205 GR, and head off. I fly down Miklabraut Road, follow the Hringbraut turnabout, and head over to the roundabout between the old cemetery and the National Museum. There, I turn off at South Street, where it stretches in a perfect line toward the perfect cone of Mount Keilir, far on the Southern Peninsula but clearly visible, like a bonsai version of Mount Fuji. I aim the car in the middle of the street; the lines point directly at the blue triangle that cools my eyes and gives me strength. "A pyramid in the desert, erected for no one!" the poet Hannes Peturson wrote. I recite a part of the "Time and Water" poem while the clipped road lines disappear under the hood.

> On a perpendicular surface
> between the circle and the cone
> grows the white flower of death.

South Street is the perpendicular area between the roundabout and the perfect cone of Keilir. I look for the white flower of death, but see nothing but white rocks on the side of the road and decide to take a closer look in the fall, when the psychedelic mushrooms start popping up.

It isn't hard to find Gunnlod's house. It stands like an un-painted crag in the middle of a garden. No smooth masonry on the outside, but rather irregular, as when Spanish houses are caulked and it's obvious that an architect was given free rein. The garden is huge and untended, filled with dandelion and angelica. Definitely plenty of snails here, I think.

The approach to the house was rather odd. Shreds of freshly cut hedge twirled over the path to the door, which looked like someone had drilled a large hole in the wall, but since I consider myself an artist, I have the utmost respect for creative architecture.

Gunnlod stood by the front door, fiddling with a sculpture. She looked up and brushed a lock of hair from her eyes.

"Hello," she said. "Are you Arnar?"

"Yeah, hello." I tried to sound like a poet.

She asked me in for coffee. Inside, all the walls were covered in books, and such books! First editions of works from the most influential authors in the history of literature. Where books weren't covering the walls, there were artworks from different eras and nations, a statue of a fertility goddess, Egyptian hieroglyphs, and some abstract paintings.

Gunnlod was close to forty and looked exactly like one would like one's own woman to look at that age. She was slim but mus-cular, had blue eyes and long black hair. Her breasts were just as a poet would have described them. I didn't quite know what to say, so I pretended to be deep in thought and put on my philosopher face.

"Have you been writing long?" she asked, breaking the silence.

"Yeah, a few years," I say.

"You've been doing quite well. Good reviews. And you seem really productive."

"Yeah, I guess I have a great inner need."

"I like how you write about nature. Apparently, it still has a place for young writers."

"Yeah, I wrote a little about the country and nature in my first book, where I used its nuances to indicate emotional mood changes."

"And in the maelstrom of emotion, you gallop around on Pegasus, right?" she said, emoting and playing up a storm.

"Yes, that is exactly when I try to ride the stallion of poetic inspiration."

"You don't ride the muse of poetry, do you?" she asked and hit me hard on the shoulder, laughing loudly.

"Ha, ha. No," I reply.

"It was actually a different kind of nature that I found so enchanting in your short story collection," she then said.

"You didn't think it went too far?" I ask, and blush a little.

"No, I don't think so. The book was just great! You've got this poetic imagination. Your lovemaking descriptions were searing hot. I was on fire."

"Th-th-thanks," I said, and blush even more.

"Would you like some more coffee?"

"Yeah, sure," I said.

"How do you get all those erotic ideas? You've hardly executed all this yourself?"

I had actually often thought to myself whether some of the moves were even possible.

"Ha, ha. I don't know . . . yeah . . . sure," I say.

"Like when the couple were in the plane and had sex with leather straps on, or when the male and female sports teams accidentally shared a shower after practice. Do athletes really have that kind of endurance?"

"I think so."

"Do you practice any sports?" she then asked.

"I use a tanning bed sometimes," I stammer.

"You really have drunk quite a lot from the mead of poetry, kiddo! You practically speak in odes," she said and fetched more coffee.

"At least, I think my fellow writers would agree I didn't get the part of court fool," I say, trying to keep up my end of the humorous stream of intelligent bantering.

She leaned over me and poured the coffee into my cup. Her breasts brushed against the back of my head, just as when a female math teacher helps with solving an equation. Her cheek touched mine, and she smelled like birch after a rain shower. A glen in Thorsmork.

"I liked the story 'Anti-gravity Love' the best. I've always dreamed of making love while floating in the air."

She stroked herself all over and danced like she was free from gravity, until she plopped down and pulled me with her. I landed on my back with her on top of me and felt her warm breath. Behind her provocative smile were white teeth and a fiery red tongue. My heart was beating fast. I tried to control myself. Darn if the woman wasn't trying to seduce me. Just because she was rather beautiful, was I expected to jump into bed with her like a groupie? I closed my eyes. Counted to ten. Counted to twenty. Thought about agricultural exports. I have always maintained a mysterious distance to women in order to perpetually nurture a poetic broken heart. When I was in love, I adored the girl from afar and waited until someone else got her. Then I would rush home and compose grief-filled love poems. I was often able to sustain the misery for a few weeks if I was careful. When I opened my eyes, I was standing naked in the middle of the living room. Her hands and feet crawled over my body like snakes. I couldn't resist this enticing snake body. I was about to ask her to stop but then noticed I had two tongues in my mouth, because she had snuck hers in. I stumbled over her teeth. Finally all resistance vanished. We partook of forbidden fruits, drank wine, and made love continuously for the next three days.

On the third day, I arose from the bed feeling a little queasy. All that food and drink and all this movement were wreaking havoc on my stomach, so I accidentally puked into an ancient-looking urn that was next to the bed.

"Forgive me," I sighed. "If it's ruined, I'll buy you another one. Boðn. Is that an expensive label?"

"No, not at all, it's just an old piece of junk," she said and smiled at me sweetly. "You can just mow the lawn instead."

I went outside to start mowing, but my machine was broken. I've never had much of a knack for machinery and had dreaded the day it would inevitably break. Gunnlod lent me a manual scythe instead. The man who had once owned it was long dead and gone. I worked on cutting grass the entire day, and she sat by the window writing.

The garden was large and difficult, surely a month's worth of labor for one man with this implement. That evening I went to meet my fellow poets and asked them for some help. They showed little interest until I told them the whole story.

The next day, all nine of us showed up, armed with scythes, and started cutting the grass. The job was harder than we had expected, and we had never seen such growth before. The work was thus delayed and stretched into weeks, but mostly it was delayed because Gunnlod regularly stepped outside and invited one of us in for "coffee," and he then wasn't seen again for three days. We grinned at each other. "She's so easy, that one," we said.

Whether it was her waterbed's fault or the fruit's, everyone vomited and got sick on the third day. But it was a small sacrifice for this phenomenal experience. Gunnlod eventually rescued her old urns and replaced them with an old kettle that the last three poets used.

But this garden was somewhat different from other gardens, and not nearly as tedious to mow. We discussed at great length why that might be. Some of the guys said the moss was softer and wetter, but I pointed out that the grass had yellowing roots, because it was overgrown. Others thought it was due to too many dandelions and angelica roots.

It's difficult to know exactly what was in Gunnlod's garden that made it different from all other gardens. We met regularly to discuss her grass, perhaps over beer, and new interesting angles popped up. We often spiced up the conversation by talking about cars, Princess Diana, and Pamela Anderson, or whether to get a stripper to entertain us. Only one of us still writes. He is rather good and always brings a dirty limerick to every meeting.

None of us got to enjoy Gunnlod, the poetess, ever again. We still kept tending to her garden, and once in a while we saw famous poets or scholars pay her a visit for three days. She's a nympho, like Madonna, we thought to ourselves. Her fame increased, and she could even be seen in gossip mags, with foreigners at her side. It said there that she had been awarded tons of money for some Nobel Prize or something.

Translated by Sola Bjarnadóttir O'Connell

The Black Dog

GYRÐIR ELÍASSON

I T WAS LATE IN THE EVENING when I drove up to the hostel in the woods. It was a large log cabin with white window frames, and it gave me the feeling I was in a foreign country.

The hostel was called the Black Dog. I had a black dog that had been by my side for quite some time, but it was invisible. There was no sign on the house, but a note written in a marker on a piece of plastic-covered paper was tacked on the log wall by the front door. I had found the house on the Internet before I set off. Perhaps it was the name that attracted me, I don't know, or the promise of a night's stay in the woods. Possibly both.

A dim bulb lit the entrance hall; the floor was dark-red clay tile. A woman soon descended the stairs at the end of the hallway. She walked toward me and greeted me and told me she was the proprietor there. I said I had a reservation, and she walked with me and showed me the room. This was a pleasant little room, with a double bed and a TV set, but the bathroom was out in the hall across from the room. Then she showed me the breakfast area, which was in a small corner, rather dark. This was a fairly young woman with a dark-blond pixie haircut and thin, with strange eyes. I suspected she could see the black dog with those eyes.

She walked up the stairs and closed a door behind her. I went back into the room and closed my door. She had mentioned there were foreign travelers in the other five rooms, and I thought it odd that so many rooms were filled this early in the year in such an out-of-the-way place. The house was dead silent. I heard nothing from any of the supposed other occupants. Maybe they were out walking in the woods, even though it was late.

I turned on the lamp by the bed. It shed soft, comfortable light. Then I opened my small bag and removed a book that I had brought with me. It was a memoir that the foster daughter of the writer T. F. Powys had written about him. She frequently mentioned his mysterious headaches and the damp room where he spent many hours during the winters reading Shakespeare. This room here was as far from being damp as any room could possibly be. It was warm and comfortable, and the trees outside the window were just turning green.

I turned on the TV, which was attached to a black rack high up on the wall. There was an old movie with Donald Sutherland playing. The reception was terrible, so I quickly turned it off. I went out in the hall with my toothbrush and into the bathroom. The floor tiles were cold, and the lightbulb above the mirror flickered frantically. It didn't seem to bode well to me.

When I came back into the room, I went straight to bed, lay down on the side closer to the lamp, and picked up the book about T. F. Powys again and continued reading. Powys lived way out in the country in England, hardly sold any of his writing while he was alive, and considered himself a failure as a writer. He had ceased writing by the time his foster daughter was growing up, and he never wrote a single word during her entire childhood, which she described in great detail. She told of the rare visits from his brother, John Cowper, and how he was hunched over and strange with his walking stick that he constantly swung around while the brothers went for long, eccentric walks in the country.

I read for a while and then put the book on the night table. Turned off the lamp, lay in the dusk of this spring evening, content with being alone, far from everyone I knew. Sleep came gradually, and I started having unsettling dreams—a lake filled with gray boats that resembled Volkswagens more than boats.

I was startled by a sound. I looked at the clock and saw it was 3:00 a.m. It came from the floor above, where the owner lived—a scratching on the wooden floor and a rather loud howling. Then everything was silent, but after a short while it started again. There was a strange desperation in the howl that I could clearly hear down to where I was lying in bed. Again I heard scratching on the floor above.

Outside the window, songbirds were waking up from their nightly nap. Their song sounded a bit hesitant in the trees, but soon the singing was almost overpowered by the howling and scratching.

I lay perfectly still and listened.

Again silence, but then no more sounds.

I fell asleep again and had no more dreams until morning. When I awoke and looked at the clock, it was 9:00. I got dressed and went to have breakfast. It was well presented, but the coffee was from a self-serve machine, and I hate that kind of coffee. I had a cup anyway, to satisfy my caffeine need. No one else was around having breakfast, and I didn't hear any of the other guests, neither coughs nor sighs.

The proprietress was nowhere to be seen.

After breakfast I went out for a walk to refresh myself before the impending long drive ahead. In the yard sat a fat white cat looking a lot like a snowdrift left behind when winter decided to leave. It sat motionless on a pile of sand that was clearly meant for children to play in, evidenced by a few colorful toy shovels. I walked up to the cat and petted him. He didn't flinch but looked up at me slyly and then closed his eyes and burrowed into the sand like he was getting ready for a nap.

The weather was pretty nice, dry and still but rather cloudy. The forest was visible from the yard, because the house was up on a hill. Below was the big lake, but I didn't see any boats like the ones in my dream.

I walked up the path closest to the house and into the lush birch woods. Here and there in between the birch trees were a few pines that were just recovering their needles. After a while I came upon a brook with a log crossing. I walked across and continued up the wooded hill. Above me the mountain towered with its crags not very tall, but strangely majestic as seen over the treetops. I heard my black dog wheezing behind me.

My cell phone rang in my jacket pocket. I cursed for not having turned it off or just left it at home before the trip. That was my wife. She was asking about how long I was planning to be away.

"I don't know," I said there in the forest, and the trees seemed to be curiously listening, reaching their branches toward me.

"Do you think you'll be back tomorrow?" she asked.

"I don't know," I repeated.

We said goodbye, in a few words as usual, and I put the phone back in my pocket, but first I considered tossing it in the brook. I think cell phones should be outlawed in forests. The two just don't go together. The voices of the woods fall silent as soon as a phone rings. I turned around and walked back, over the brook and toward the hostel. The white cat had disappeared, as if it had realized it was clearly overkill to pose in front of a hostel with this particular name. I looked into the garden to see if someone was there. The garden was empty, except it was full of trees and practically melted into the woods. I walked into the house and removed my shoes on the maroon tiles, because they were covered in dirt from the path. I went to my room and packed my things, then went up the stairs and knocked on the door by the stairway. The woman opened the door and looked at me searchingly in the semidarkness, as if she didn't know who I was. Then her expression changed. I told her I wanted to settle my bill, and she told me to go downstairs. She'd be right there. I strained to hear whether there was an animal in her room before she closed the door, but I heard nothing.

We settled our business by the table downstairs. She inserted my credit card into an old-fashioned slider and pulled the lever with a quick move. I shook her hand and thanked her for the night's stay. There was still no sign of life from the other rooms. I seemed to recall her mentioning they were Germans, some group of geologists.

I drove off and headed down the road between tall aspens. The leaves had just come in but had not yet reached full size, still pale green. Later they would turn darker and double in size or more.

I was well on my way when I realized I had left my book about the English egocentric on the nightstand. I thought it was too late to turn around and just hoped someone else would enjoy it.

My black dog snuggled in the back seat and took a snooze. I could see him clearly in the rearview mirror. For some reason, he could be seen only in mirrors. Every now and then he peered at me with one eye, like he was monitoring my driving.

Translated by Sola Bjarnadóttir O'Connell

Late Afternoon in Four Parts

BRAGI ÓLAFSSON

1

THE HOUSE NUMBER IS AN EVEN NUMBER.

Njördur, age seven, is sitting in a car seat in the back. He is on his way to visit his classmate Hlynur, and it is his mother, Hildur, who is the chauffeur.

"That's right," she says to her son.

"What?"

"That Hlynur's house number is an even number."

Njördur stares at his mother. Perhaps the inquiring look in his eyes is because it has been a while since he mentioned the house number being even. At least two or three minutes; it was just as they set out.

"But you are an odd number," says Hildur and turns around to smile at him. She has stopped the car in front of the building.

"I am not a number," says Njördur. He and Hlynur have recently learned about odd and even numbers in school.

"But you are seven. Did you bring your hat?"

"No."

"I asked you to bring it, in case you go outside to play."

"Hlynur only wants to play inside."

"Yes, but maybe his mom wants you to go outside. You will just have to borrow a hat from him if you do."

"We won't be going outside."

"What is his mother's name again?"

"I don't know."

Hildur rings the doorbell that Hlynur's mother had told her was marked only as "Friedlander" and not with their own names. She feels ashamed that she can't recall what the woman's name is. She just remembers it starts with "A." She reads the names on the other buzzers and notices that on the floor below lives a man she went to college with. It has to be him; it seems unlikely there'd be others with that very unusual name. The old classmate is a composer; it occurs to Hildur to ask Hlynur's mother what it's like to live on the floor above a composer; they probably sometimes hear music. She even formulates the question in her mind as she presses the buzzer.

"Isn't it difficult to live above a dissonant man like Jafet Ebenezar?"

But she forgets to ask, because when she sees Hlynur's mother, she notices something in her demeanor that instantly take her thoughts in another direction. Hildur stands in the doorway while Njördur squeezes by her to run up the stairs, without as much as a goodbye; A is on the second-floor landing, alone—and somewhat forlorn.

In the car on the way, Hildur asked herself why she didn't remember seeing Hlynur's mom at the school, or whether it was possible that his father had taken on the role of guardian at PTA meetings and other functions that demanded parental presence (Hildur herself had limited interest in that part of her son's education). But she knew Hlynur's father didn't live with him and his mom. Besides, she thought it unlikely that the father had an active interest in raising his son for some reason.

When she and A greet each other in the stairwell, Hildur

quickly realizes that A is not a very chatty person. But it is, of course, possible she is just in a bad mood at the moment. She has rather short auburn hair and is wearing a tight black dress and burgundy slippers; and Hildur wonders whether the tobacco smell she senses in the hallway comes from her, Hlynur's mom, or is simply a permanent odor that is always there.

"Njördur, darling!" Hildur shouts. "Aren't you going to say goodbye to me?"

Njördur calls something out to his mother from the floor above, and, as always—she can't help it—Hildur imagines that this is the last time she will hear her son, that something terrible is about to happen.

"Promise to behave," she says, more to herself but at least loud enough for him to hear. Then she turns to A and says, "I should be back here around five?"

"To pick him up?" A seems to be startled.

"Yeah, maybe just before five?"

A nods her head with a wan smile.

"Pardon me," says Hildur, "but I am so bad with names. What was yours again?"

A stares at Hildur for a moment, long enough for Hildur to wonder if she even knows it herself. Did she forget her own name? Why is she taking so long to reply?

But then she answers. She says her name is Agnes. She doesn't seem to want to say anything else but gets ready to head up the stairs. Hildur was going to ask her if they should exchange phone numbers but figures she can always find her online, now that she knows the woman's name.

"Well," she says. "I will be back later."

"Yes," says Agnes, then suddenly remembers something. "But . . . but he . . . ?" she asks.

"He? Do you mean . . . ?"

"Yes."

"Do you mean Njördur?"

"Yeah. I'm not good with names either," says Agnes and smiles again like it is an alien gesture.

"Yes, it is Njördur." Hildur wants to say something more—she is suddenly filled with unease—but there is no further opportunity to chat; this is how their first conversation ends.

It has started to rain by the time she gets out on the sidewalk, and she recalls her son's words about their not going outside to play, just staying in. Friendly boy, Hlynur, she thinks to herself and vaguely recalls him from an after-school session for the kids in their classroom. She hadn't really thought about it then, but wondered afterward why she hadn't seen Hlynur's parents.

Odd how some children have so little in common with their parents, she thinks when she gets into her car. That does indeed seem to be the case with Hlynur and his mother, Agnes.

2

AN OCTOGENARIAN LADY LIVES in the basement apartment of Agnes and Hlynur's building. When Hildur approached the house, she had noticed her through the window, which was half underground, as if the street surface and the sidewalk had soared since the time it was first erected. The old woman sat at her kitchen table looking toward the wall above the stove; it was a white wall, which made Hildur wonder why there was nothing on the wall; why don't people generally have art on their kitchen walls?

On Hildur's kitchen wall, to the left of the stove, for instance, is a drawing by a younger Njördur that he made in school. It is of a man standing on top of the Eiffel Tower, and beneath it is written, in large uneven letters, "Padua." This picture has always elated Hildur—that is why it is on the wall—and she thinks about it while she drives away from the house. When Njördur brought it home from school, she asked him why he had written "Padua," but he wasn't able to explain it.

She thought the Italian city name was just as adorable as the picture itself.

A few minutes after Hildur left Njördur at Hlynur's, the old lady in the basement knocks on Agnes's door. She asks whether that guy downstairs—meaning the composer—disturbed her the night before.

"No," says Agnes.

"It took me forever to fall asleep," says the old lady.

"He wasn't playing all that late, was he?" asks Agnes.

"Late?"

"Late into the night."

"Well, I had a hard time falling asleep. But it's quiet up here at your place," she says.

"Quiet?"

"You don't make much noise."

"Hlynur's classmate is visiting."

"Oh?" The lady livens up. "Can I help with anything?"

"Help?"

"They might want some cake? I think I have some coffee cake left over from yesterday."

But Agnes turns it down and hints politely that they want to be left alone now; she has some work to tend to that is due after the weekend.

"Just send him down to my place, little Hlynur, if you need more peace and quiet," says the old lady. "He can come down when his buddy leaves."

"I will mention it to him," say Agnes, and they take leave.

3

HILDUR DECIDES TO USE THE TWO HOURS Njördur is with Hlynur to go to the bank. She knows one branch is open until six on Fridays. Then she is going to do some shopping for the weekend.

When she gets to the bank, it is unusually busy, and according to the number she gets, she is fifteenth in line. "You are fifteenth in line" echoes in her head. She thinks about the music that invariably plays when customers call company phone lines. "You are number fourteen in the line." Then there is music for a couple of minutes, and then the voice again: "You are number thirteen in the line." Continuing on this tangent, Hildur's mind goes to thinking about Jafet Ebenezar, her old classmate; how would he react if he were waiting with a phone pressed against his ear listening to Icelandic pop music between announcements of his place in line? "You are number twelve in the line." He probably never calls a service line, she thinks to herself. And she wonders if he ever speaks to Agnes, who lives above him? Strange man, this Jafet Ebenezar. Just like the name. Never knew him to live with a woman, she muses. Wonder if he slept with Agnes? Why am I thinking that? Why not? It is just normal to think that. These are people of similar age. Both single, as far as I know. But did it happen? she asks herself, all the while watching the screen above the counters. It would have been an awkward encounter, she answers herself. Is that why Hlynur's mom is so timid? Does she know Jafet and I were at school together? No, she wouldn't sleep with a guy like him. Or rather, he wouldn't sleep with her. His wife is the music. The difficult music. Never heard—probably no one has heard it on the radio. Let alone on TV. Jafet Ebenezar and television are two factors that don't belong in the same calculation. Jafet Ebenezar doesn't have a TV. Yes, he definitely does. He watches it every night. All day. He has access to a special channel that pumps out classical music 24/7. In the unlikely event that Jafet should turn out to be the composer of the ditty that plays in this bank's commercials, then I wouldn't even know. Such things are never mentioned. But this bank is always promoting itself on TV. Hildur spots colorful balls in a basket in the middle of the floor. They are the size of baseballs, with the bank's name and logo. And they are free. People can grab a ball if they want. She sees a young man, waiting to be served just like her, snatch one; and she starts to think about getting one herself. And when she sees another person follow the young man's example, she decides to follow suit.

She gets two balls, one for Njördur and another for Hlynur. These balls seem to be rather well made. She wonders if Hlynur would like to get it as a present. What kind of toys does he have? Maybe he is not allowed to dribble a ball in the apartment; it might disturb the composer downstairs. Well, then maybe they should not allow Jafet to play his instrument. Which instrument does he play? Hildur calls up an image in her head of Jafet at a school party in college, where he played the guitar. But that he would be playing a guitar today is as unimaginable as . . . as unimaginable as what? She puts the balls in her purse. "You are number eleven in the line." She notices a man sitting on a leather bench close to the front door; he is holding a paper cup of coffee, which, like the balls, also has the bank's logo. You can get free coffee here from a large, pretty coffeemaker in the back of the waiting area. Hildur sees the man is about to fall asleep. His head falls forward and he brings it up a tad, but then it falls forward again; she starts to worry that he will drop the cup on the floor. "You are number ten in line." The man with the coffee is probably number one in line, without having any idea. Maybe it was his turn a while ago and his number has expired. How much longer does Njördur have left of his playdate? An hour and fifteen minutes. Hildur is going to the store afterward. She was going to buy something for him, some little toy, but now that she got the ball for nothing, she feels that might be enough; maybe just something sweet for dessert, even though she thinks he will probably get something sweet at Hlynur's house.

"You are number nine in line."

She *is* number nine in line.

And then it happens: the sleepy man's cup falls to the floor and the man comes to.

4

THE SUN IS SHINING AGAIN when Hildur goes to pick up
Njördur. When she parks by the house, she notices the front door is
open, and when she gets to the door, she sees a newspaper has been
lodged in the crack to keep it open. Before she enters, she sneaks
a peak at the old lady to see if she is still sitting in her kitchen, but
doesn't see her—just the blank wall. Should I ring the buzzer or
just go upstairs and knock? she asks herself, then decides to go up
without ringing the buzzer. She feels like that will be a friendlier
approach while also showing that she trusts Agnes to care for her
own offspring. It is never a given to entrust one's belongings to
strangers, let alone one's children. She walks through the door and
wonders a bit about how worn the stairwell is.

The pale-yellow walls—white in places—remind Hildur of the
apartment building she lived in as a child. The paint is peeling, not
just in one place but in many.

When she gets to Jafet's landing, she is tempted to put her ear
to the door that bears the composer's initials. Why just the initials?
But she doesn't hear a thing when she tries to listen. At least no
music (as she was hoping for). As she continues up the stairs, she
hears someone inside his door—presumably Jafet himself—loudly
clearing his throat.

She stops cold on the stairs. It has been a long time since she
has heard from her old classmate. Not that she heard much from
him at college either, but still: it has been decades since she has
heard from this man. The throat clearing goes on. No music, just
throat sounds, thinks Hildur. How long ago since we graduated?
She imagines Jafet sitting at a piano this very moment, trying to
decide where to put his fingers. Which two notes go together the
least; which sound will annoy a listener the most?

But what listener?

There is no music. Jafet just clears his throat instead. He
doesn't realize that he does have a listener this moment, just

outside his door, a person who knows who he is and who could put the music he would play for her—if he would just think of playing something this moment—into a certain context. But the opportunity slips away.

He stops clearing his throat.

Hildur continues up the stairs.

Outside Agnes and Hlynur's door is a straw mat with the word WELCOME on it and a few pairs of shoes, and Hildur sees they are all boy's shoes except for one pair, which must belong to the mother. A basket full of sweaters and coats is next to the door, and under the pile she spots the same kind of ball she got at the bank. They have been to the bank already, she thinks. But she decides to still give Hlynur the ball. She hesitates for a second before she knocks; she wants to eavesdrop, to see if she can hear the boys inside. But she doesn't hear a thing.

She knocks.

"Hello," she says when Agnes comes to the door, still wearing the same tight dress as before (had she expected her to change her clothes?).

"Hello," says Agnes.

Njördur comes to the door.

"Well, little man. Did you have a good time?"

Njördur nods hesitantly, then shrugs his shoulders. Then he comes out the door and puts on his shoes.

"Did you say good-bye to Hlynur, darling?"

Njördur puts his coat on, then watches his mother in silence, who looks at Agnes apologetically. Hildur takes the ball from her purse and hands it to Agnes while pointing to the balls in the basket.

"I see you already have one, but it is OK to have two. I was just at the bank before."

"Oh?" Agnes thanks her and takes the ball.

"Thank Agnes," says Hildur to Njördur, and he shakes her hand muttering "Thanks," so quietly she can barely hear it. "You will meet again on Monday," she adds cheerfully, and Agnes nods her head.

Hildur was going to mention Jafet, but this time she didn't forget, she decided to let it be.

Wonder if he will clear his throat again? she asks herself on the way down the stairs, but hears nothing.

"Well, little man. I brought you a ball, too."

The sun is gone by the time they are outside.

"Did you have a good time?" asks Hildur again when Njördur is strapped into his car seat. "Didn't you?" she persists.

Njördur doesn't respond. It isn't until they have turned a corner that he expresses himself about the playdate.

"Hlynur wasn't there," he says.

"What do you mean?"

"Only his mom was home."

"Did Hlynur leave before I came to get you? I thought it was a little strange that he didn't see you to the door."

"He wasn't home at all."

"What do you mean 'at all'? You weren't alone with his mother, were you?"

"Yeah."

Hildur stops the car in a spot between two cars and looks back at her son.

"Were you alone with his mom?" she repeats.

"Yes."

"Are you telling me the truth?"

Njördur nods his head in agreement.

"I have to drive back there," Hildur says determinedly, and puts the car in gear.

"No, don't do that," Njördur begs her.

"What do you mean? I have to talk to the woman."

"Don't do it, Mommy."

Hildur switches back to neutral and looks at her son for a short while.

"And what were you doing?" she asks.

"She was just in the kitchen."

"Didn't she speak to you?"

"No. She just told me to go to Hlynur's room."

"Did she do something to you?" Hildur pushes.

Njördur shakes his head.

"Are you absolutely sure?"

"Yes," he says.

"Do you know what I mean when I ask you if she did anything to you?"

Njördur shakes his head, and Hildur regards him for a while.

"Where was Hlynur?"

"I don't know."

"Did she give you anything?"

"No, she didn't give me anything."

"No milk or anything to drink?"

"She gave me some juice."

"And no food?"

"I didn't want anything. She told me there was some old lady in the basement who wanted to give me cake."

"Oh, my god," sighs Hildur. "I must call her when we get home."

They don't discuss the playdate any further for the rest of the way home, but she hugs him when they get out of the car and asks him to wait in his room while she makes the call. Then she locates Agnes's number but hesitates before keying it in.

Agnes takes a long time to answer.

"Hello," says Hildur. "This is Hildur, Njördur's mom. He just told me that he was alone with you."

"We were both here," Agnes replies.

"He told me Hlynur wasn't even home."

"No, he went to his uncle."

"But didn't he invite him over?"

"His uncle had invited him over. I just forgot."

"No, I meant didn't Hlynur invite him over?"

"His uncle?"

"Njördur."

"Yes."

"But why . . . ? I don't understand this."

"There was a change," says Agnes.

"Change?" Hildur's voice is getting louder. "And what was he doing there, then?"

"I showed him Hlynur's toys."

"I might have wanted to know about this."

"Know?"

"That your son wasn't home."

"Isn't he home?"

"Who? Njördur?"

"Yes."

"I just picked him up."

"I know that. But pardon me, the lady from downstairs is knocking on my door. You have to excuse me for a minute."

Hildur sighs and waits for Agnes to get back on the phone. But she has to wait quite a while; and after she hears a door slam in the apartment on the other end of the line, she waits on the line longer still, so long that she finally decides to hang up and let Agnes do her thing, as she puts it in her mind.

"Isn't he home?" What the hell did she mean by that?

Hildur goes to Njördur's room; the door is ajar, and she peeks in.

Njördur is sitting on the floor; he has his back to the door and appears to be playing. Hildur looks at him for a while, but when he lifts his head, she pulls back. Best not to startle him. But she keeps an eye on him, and he doesn't seem to be making an effort to stand up or turn around; he is watching the wall. It is the only empty wall in his room. It used to have pictures of some space aliens, but he had suddenly lost interest in aliens. He looks at the wall for so long that Hildur decides that the right thing to do is to just leave him alone. She thinks to herself that he will be doing something other than staring at the wall when she returns after a while. And then she will knock on the door and clear her throat, so he won't be startled.

Translated by Sola Bjarnadóttir O'Connell

SMS from Catalonia

AUÐUR AVA ÓLAFSDÓTTIR

H E'S ON THE PHONE and tells me he's stuck inside a stationary bus that set off for the mountain village more than an hour ago. He says he tried to be one of the first on the coach to grab a seat in the left row, to avoid having to look down at the steep drop below and risk throwing up the chicken quiche he bought at the airport, and which had probably gotten stale anyway. I know I don't seem like the acrophobic type, he adds, being 6 feet 1½ inches tall. It's 91 degrees outside and stuffy on the bus, and the driver has cut out to take a leak, or so it is assumed, because he pulled over on the side of a tortuous country road without warning and then vanished into the darkness. But that was forty minutes ago, and the final has started. He'd planned on reaching the village in good time to watch it on a crappy TV in a bar somewhere with a cold beer and deep-fried calamari between his fingers, but now suspects that it's the driver who's doing that right now. He says he misses me and that my fingerprints are still visible on his tummy and other parts of his flesh, but right now he wants to know if I could do him a huge favor while he's waiting for the driver to return. He fully realizes that he's asking for a lot, because he knows I never watch soccer, but would there be any chance, my lover of five months asks me, of you turning on your TV in Reykjavík to watch the live match with just one eye and text me every now and then, maybe four or five times in all, ten would be great, as the game unfolds. Especially when something important happens, like when a team scores, and preferably the number of the player, he would really appreciate that, because it would really put him in the picture, stuck as he is on a clammy bus with a bunch of strangers and their shopping bags. My team is in red and yellow, he says, and the others are in white. There are eleven players on each side, unless someone gets sent off for fouling. Sorry for asking you to do this, he says, I'm sure you'd prefer to watch a documentary about melting ice caps on the other side, if I know you right. Speaking of which, today I saw the first star after my twenty-eight nightless summer nights on your enchanted island, not that the light was the only thing keeping me awake, sweetheart. Even though I'd been glued to a Danish documentary about circumcision in Africa when my lover phoned, I want him to know that there is virtually nothing I wouldn't do for him, stranded on a bus like that with food poisoning in 91 degrees, or even if he were anywhere else, for that matter. I promptly switch the channel and immediately realize that the red-and-yellow guys are running faster than the white ones, which gives me something nice to text him about in my first message. Next, I tell him the red-and-yellows are still chasing the ball, and so are the whites. When I quote the commentator as saying that number 7 of the red-and-yellows is in a good strategic position, he thanks me for letting him know, and I sense he might be telling me he's happy. Next, I tell him that number 4 of the white team's eyebrow is being stitched as maroon blood gushes out of an open vein and his eyelashes are fluttering like the red wings of a butterfly and he's covered in blood. Thanks, and then? he asks. Nimble pass from a white player, I write. Good, he answers. A white guy kicks a red-and-yellow guy, causing him to fall on the Astroturf, curled up in a fetal position and crying, I write. Ouch, he answers, is he out of the game? The red-and-yellow number 11 kicks the white number 9 in the stomach, I write. Is he faking it or did he deserve it? He asks. I tell him the red-and-yellow number 11 has just scored 1–0 this very second and that he has golden hair. Please continue, he answers, please, I love you. I tell him in the tenth and final text that the whites have been given one last free kick, but the whistle was blown and the red-and-yellows are hopping up and down on the grass and singing. He calls again when I've turned the TV off and am running a bath. I sense from his quivering voice that he's been through a life-changing experience. He was so grateful for my texts, he tells me, I made it all so real and beautiful for him, he'd never really thought of the colors like that before; the red blood and green grass and how one amplified the other, and then the golden hair against the black sky, and he wants me to know that he is so terribly, terribly fond of me and misses me. He tells me that the driver has finally returned, smelling of booze. They still have the canyon ahead, but he's feeling much better now, and if he ever survives this, he'd be willing to marry me. In any case, he says, I'll bring the hammock when I come to the island, as we discussed. You can tie one end to the weeping willow and the other to the clothesline post by the bins. It'll be shaped like butterfly wings, violet with yellow dots, because that goes so well with your porcelain skin.

Translated by Brian FitzGibbon

A Pen Changes Hands

ÓSKAR ÁRNI ÓSKARSSON

FOUR OR FIVE YEARS AGO, I attended a poetry festival in Akureyri, along with six other poets. The reading took place in Gilið, to great acclaim from the attending locals. I had forgotten my pen up at the hotel but needed to jot something down before my turn came at the podium. A colleague sitting next to me loaned me his pen, a cheap type of Biro. As sometimes happens, I inadvertently put the pen in my pocket after having used it. It wasn't until I arrived back in Reykjavík that I found I still had the poet's pen in my jacket pocket. However, since the pen wasn't an especially remarkable pen, I didn't feel it was necessary to contact the owner. Besides, I didn't really want to have anything to do with that particular poet, so I decided to adopt the pen as my own. Soon I discovered that anything I wrote with the pen showed distinct characteristics of my colleague's style, a poet I did not really admire, so I got rid of it. I seem to remember leaving it on a bench at a bus stop. Strange as it may seem, the poet in question has not published a single poem since. Stranger still, in recent years poems by a young poet have been appearing in journals, poems that show a definite stylistic resemblance to the poems by the original pen's owner. And that's not all. Last month the literary journal *Stína* published three poems in the same style, but by yet another author.

Translated by Áslaug Agnarsdóttir

The Cook

ÓSKAR MAGNÚSSON

"**T**HE OLD MAN SHOULD BE ABLE to understand that if we don't get anything to eat, then we don't fish either. This lousy cook should be fired, or I won't do another tour." It was Deckhand Hrólfur talking, directing his speech to Benni, who was chief engineer on the *Hafborg* RE. Benni listened. There was no disagreement about this; all of the crewmen would leave sooner or later if the cook wasn't changed. They'd been on night watch, and when they wanted to have a snack after the last haul, there wasn't a bite to be found anywhere, no bread or any cold cuts to put on it, not even dry biscuits. The refrigerator was locked, as well as the locker back on the boat deck. It wasn't Benni's job to look after the cook, but they often talked to him when they didn't take their complaints to the captain. Benni knew the Old Man best of all. He'd worked with him for many years and knew how to deal with him.

"We'll just wake up the cook. He's been sleeping for six hours. Hopefully he wasn't drinking before he went to bed, because then we'll be in the shit," said Engineer Benni. The cook did not sleep forward in the cabin but instead had his bunk directly under the mess, and that's where Hrólfur went. He shook Cook Dommi heartily and then ran back up again. After a moment, they heard someone stumbling on the stairs. Keys clattered, and the lock on the refrigerator was opened. Cook Dommi appeared ash gray in the door of the mess and started throwing mandarin oranges at the crew as they sat there.

"Absolutely, have something to eat; you can't go hungry, you wretches," he hissed as he shot limp and shabby mandarins all over the mess. The mandarins must have been from Christmas. Several mandarins landed on crewmembers but most on the walls and portholes. The mess was completely filthy by the time Cook Dommi finished with the mandarins, stumbled down the stairs again, and mumbled, "And I was just drifting off."

By great luck the tour was over later that day. On the return trip, Raggi the Liar found some food for the crew, but they let Dommi sleep. Besides being a liar, Raggi was first mate on the *Hafborg* RE, called the *Bogga* for short, a pleasant fellow and a fine fisherman. His face was very lined, with a jutting lower jaw, usually light-colored peach fuzz on his chin, and jutting yellowish teeth. He was splayfooted, which is generally considered good for a seaman. Raggi seldom uttered a true word but didn't realize his own flaw, and always thought he was being truthful. Thus, his stories often had the tendency to sound very precise and authentic. His nickname stuck to him except on Seaman's Day, when he was always called Ragnar the Untruthful. Raggi the Liar alternated watches with Lárus Símonarson, Lalli Sím—the Old Man. The Old Man shared ownership of the boat with his cousin, who was a highly educated doctor in marine biology. He had never gone to sea but owned a fish-processing factory out on Grandi. The *Bogga* always landed its catch at the doctor's factory.

Lalli Sím was a real sea dog. Large, thick, and gray-bearded, in a wool sweater and a knitted wool cap. He was as sharp as a lion and well read, especially in the old sagas and law. He was quiet but pleasant, and sometimes sarcastic. Lalli had been going to sea all his life, mostly on trawlers, and the *Bogga* was one of few trawlers that was outfitted from Reykjavík—169 tons but recorded as 105 so that it could fish in areas limited to boats that size. It was a productive ship with a good return, although the crew felt that the doctor didn't always pay the highest wage. They informed Lalli that they wouldn't sail again with Cook Dommi on board.

Dommi took being fired very badly, and when he walked up the pier to the coffee shop, they heard him mutter as if to himself, "Mandarins! Those idiots! Firing a guy with so much experience and not even being able to tell the difference between mandarins and clementines!"

The Old Man had trouble sleeping. He often slept very little when fishing, but usually took to his bunk on the way in. There were strict orders not to wake him even when the boat reached the harbor. He could sleep twelve hours at one go in the harbor. He was never in a rush to get home—the kids had all left home, and the wife would rather have him sleep on the boat than come home unrefreshed.

Captain Lárus Símonarson woke up rested and cheerful this May morning and walked up the pier. He met a clean-cut boy, pale-colored and slim, who asked whether he had room for a deckhand. Lalli told it like it was, that all he needed was a cook. The boy said that he'd been thinking about becoming a deckhand—he didn't know how to cook at all but had been on trawlers two summers and once at Christmas.

Lalli had no need to put an inexperienced cook on such a productive ship, but he was in a good mood and felt like giving the boy a try. "It's excellent that you've been to sea—we'll need you on deck, too, since we've only got eight up there. Take note, good fellow: the cook gets one and a quarter, not just one share like the deckhands. Why shouldn't you be able to cook like the others? Who's your mother?" After the boy listed his relatives on his mother's side and Lalli decided she was descended from a long line of famous cooks, they went down to the ship to have a look at things.

One entered the mess through the galley, which was as large as the guest bathroom in a normal single-family house.

All the same, they made their agreement there in the mess.

Ómar Matthíasson, a nineteen-year-old student in the Reykjavík Lyceum, was hired as cook on the *Hafborg* RE. He was to report for work in approximately one week, when the boat would be finished undergoing repairs. "Now go home to your mother, and cook meals morning and night for a week. That'll do, since we never stay out longer than a week at a time. Be happy, man."

One and a quarter, cook, one and a quarter, thought Ómar.

When they left the harbor a week later, the weather was gloomy. Ómar tied on his apron as they steamed out. Mother had made him a number of aprons by sewing ties to dish towels and exhorted him to always wear a clean one. "Change your apron once a day, my dear Ói," she said. "Then you should start by serving meatballs, at least once during the first twenty-four-hour period, or the meat will go bad."

Ómar started with the meatballs—he wasn't going to take any chances with the raw ingredients. He spread out the meat mixture in its plastic, melted margarine in the pan, and dipped his spoon in it so the mixture wouldn't stick to the spoon as he made the meatballs. The pitching of the ship increased steadily, and although Ómar had previously been at sea, it was almost a year since the last time. He was also nervous. He was feeling queasy: seasickness was starting to rear its ugly head. He continued making meatballs; he had to make a heap of them for eight men, or seven anyway—he himself wouldn't eat much now. And then the gushing started. The new cook (at one and a quarter) vomited heartily over the meat mixture. He wiped his mouth on his apron and thought that now it was do or die. He would really be in the shit if he wasn't able to produce his first meal. When Engineer Benni came walking through the galley on his way to the mess for a cup of coffee, he saw the cook scraping most of the vomit from the meat so that he could keep cooking meatballs for seven. He put an arm amicably around Ómar's shoulders. "Go to your bunk, man, we'll look after ourselves tonight."

When Ómar woke up, they were docked at the town of

Ólafsvík. That suited him fine, because they ended up sheltering there for twenty-four hours while the storm passed over. Ómar was able to put in some practice in the kitchen and on the equipment, get a good grasp on the job. He went to the shop and bought beef goulash, which he planned to cook in something of a celebration. He would even put laurel leaves in it.

It turned out the shopkeeper had sawed some lamb steaks, and he sold Ómar the bones and fat. He threw that rubbish in the sea. The ship departed again. Ómar knew precisely the fourteen dishes he had copied down from his mother in a spiral notebook with a monkey picture on the front. That was a coincidence, he thought. One of the fourteen meals quickly received the name "Piss-Warm Buffet," because in it the cook served hot and cold together. It was sausages and mashed potatoes, pickled herring, eggs, and cold meat leftovers. All of his dishes were elegantly served, with a clean tablecloth and always a clean apron. The cook followed along with the fishing, but the crew didn't feel the need to include him unless they had a pretty good haul. "Bake a sponge cake, we've got a bloody slack-fish," called out Hrólfur when the catch was small. Cook Ómar had come up with a method of reheating sponge cakes that he had bought at Nóatún Supermarket that made them seem freshly baked. The crewmen all pretended they were.

The Old Man never praised the food but sometimes said, "Holy shit, your mother must be a good cook." On Sundays it was always leg or rack of lamb. Then, the Old Man would take the remains of the rack up to the bridge and sit there gnawing and sucking the bones. After that he'd throw them in the sea. Just like the chess set. He had thrown it in the sea when his prospective son-in-law checkmated him. The man was Scottish, big and strong, but always sick. "Dizzy." He stayed only a short time on board, as well as in the family. Then the Old Man felt ashamed of himself and brought a new chessboard along on the next tour, as well as a battery for the clock in the galley. After that he informed the crew he was going bankrupt: these expenditures were going to screw him completely.

He showed them the battery and said, "One hundred and eighty," meaning that was the cost. Then he shook his head in despair. He called himself stingy and penniless, but he had enough money and was the most generous of men.

"Look at that goddamn cook. He can actually work," said Engineer Benni. They were bringing in a five-ton haul, and all hands were on deck. "We bosses don't need to be calling each other names," said the cook, who was starting to become more and more assertive. Raggi the Liar said that he could immediately calculate how much they were making on this tour, since he knew the prices of fish in and out. No one knew whether his figures were correct, because the accounts weren't settled until the fall, and by then everyone had forgotten Raggi's lies. And no one knew how the doctor calculated things either. Some said he could only divide and subtract. Raggi mostly multiplied.

Cook Ómar put dried fruit to soak in a bowl that he propped on a wet cloth on a table in the galley. The fruit-soup recipe in his notebook with the monkey cover said that the fruit needed to soak overnight. Ómar went to sleep. In the morning all of the fruit was gone except for one prune.

Ómar cooked sheep sausages for lunch, and then the soup, of course.

"What kind of garbage is this?" said the Old Man, lifting the large ladle from the soup pot. From it hung a gluey light-brown mud made of water, sugar, and potato flour.

"It's fruit soup," said Cook Ómar in the galley doorway.

"Fruit soup!" shouted the entire crew. "And where is the fruit?"

"You ate it all. You ate it while I was sleeping. Here, just like anywhere else, you can eat food up only one time, so now you decide when you want to eat it! And I'm not locking the fridge or locker up anymore—take what you want. And let the Old Man have the prune if you can find it." They seemed to get the message. Some of them had a blob of the gluey rubbish, with cream on top.

Cook Ómar had become one of them. He shared with them his

dreams of becoming a priest in the countryside and having a wife and plenty of children. In return they called him a mama's boy and Jesus child and said he'd never amount to anything more than a lusty, drunken rural priest in some isolated valley somewhere. More than likely he'd be defrocked. The atmosphere on board was very friendly. The cook and Deckhand Hrólfur had become particularly good comrades. They were standing astern when the net was let out.

"Ommi, wouldn't it be fun to go down with the trawl door and see how it works down there?" asked Hrólfur.

"Yeah, maybe, if you go first," said Ómar. "Where's your engagement ring?"

"Gauja and I broke up a long time ago," said Hrólfur. "I just didn't take it off until last Saturday. I pawned it off to a cab driver. Got two bottles of aquavit for it. I'm not sure I'll go get it back."

They stopped talking. Ómar looked at the trawl door and Hrólfur at his finger, and then he said, "Maybe I should try and work things out with her before I turn thirty. She's great. She wanted us to buy an apartment together. She told me I needed to lose some weight."

"Your turn to sleep. Do you want me to wake you up for dinner?"

"What've you got?" asked Hrólfur.

"Breaded cutlets."

"Yeah, wake me up for the breading," said Hrólfur, and he went to the cabin.

The fall low-pressure systems had arrived. The *Bogga* had been docked for two days at the village of Rif with a good catch that the doctor was waiting for. They had nothing to do, just sat in the mess. The Old Man stumped the cook on the old sagas. Raggi the Liar had decided to become a truck driver and immediately claimed that he'd earn a wage many times that of a ship captain. Hrólfur sat in the other corner and talked to Engineer Benni.

"I'm not going to go pick up the ring unless I get Gauja first," he said. Benni agreed. "Things have got to be done in the right order."

The Old Man had had enough of hanging around. "Let's tie up, we're going to punch it home," he said. He added coffee to his cup and went up to the bridge to check the weather.

Cook Ómar was pretty worried on the way home. Never had he experienced such weather. They alternated watches, but Ómar didn't dare go down when his watch was finished. It was safer to stay near the Old Man. He couldn't tell from looking at him if they were in danger. The Old Man just peered into the darkness and didn't say a single unnecessary word. The *Bogga* drudged along for hours. No one had any appetite. They had stopped drinking coffee, just sat in the mess and held on, except for Ómar. He was up on the bridge.

Finally the Old Man looked at Ómar and said, "I'm going to pledge a hundred thousand krónur to the Stranda Church if we survive this." The young man's heart stopped for a moment—were they actually in any real danger, or what? No reply. The Old Man had stopped talking again.

When Ómar Matthíasson, the cook, lightheartedly hopped onto land holding the end of the rope and tied it to the pier by the coffee shop, the Old Man stuck his head, with its knitted cap still in place, out the bridge window and said, "Can't a guy even tell a joke around here?"

Translated by Philip Roughton

Travel Companion

RÚNAR VIGNISSON

Reykjavík, July 11

S HE SET OFF FOR THE WESTFJORDS EARLIER. Shouldn't take her more than three to four hours to get to the village of Drangsnes now that the roads are so good. Hopefully she'll drive carefully and can see well enough with her puffy eyes.

This evening she can enjoy eating with her traveling companions. Fresh fish from the village, if all goes according to plan. Maybe halibut, maybe haddock; she won't want cod. Then she can go and sit in the hot tub down by the shoreline before she goes to sleep. Will certainly take half a sleeping pill after all the things that have happened.

Red splashes over all the walls, it'd better not dry and harden.

July 12

TEXT MESSAGE, 07:42: "We're setting off if u'd like to know."

They clearly don't intend to take more than an hour and a half in getting from Drangsnes to the pier in Norðurfjörður. Should have got there about nine to load the boat. A traveling group of fifteen will have quite a bit of accompanying luggage. Well, fourteen, actually.

It's one of the most majestic driving routes. The Kalbaksvík Inlet, for example, with cliffs on all sides. A man once plunged from them while rounding up sheep and wasn't found until the snow melted the following spring.

And the inlet of Trékyllisvík. A pastoral poem in itself.

The meteorologist in the group had arranged for a good sea passage, so this will be a pleasant sailing trip. Innumerable things to see on the way, not least the further north they get. The sheer sides of Drangaskörð are beautiful when seen from the ocean, not to mention the sea cliffs of Hornbjarg and Hælavíkurbjarg. She won't be seasick today, not even afraid to sail. Shouldn't get bored, either, with all those intelligent and amusing people around her. Maybe a bit by herself, all the same.

She'll have reached Hornvík Inlet by noon, to commune directly with the soul-nourishing soil, as some philosopher expressed it just now on the radio. According to the weather forecast, the sea's smooth and calm, hardly a ripple on the surface. It's magnificent to arrive at this oasis between two majestic cliffs on a day like this. In a travel guides it says that when people arrive and it's bright daylight all night, all of wildlife is busy nesting, breeding, growing, and blooming. They're so enchanted by these primeval powers that they return completely refreshed. Maybe reformed, too.

They'll come ashore just further along from Langikambur and begin by walking out on the rocky promontory that stretches a few dozen yards out into the inlet. No edging out onto it for those who are unsteady on their feet or have a fear of heights. But she'll manage easily and, you never know, she might even have lunch out on its furthest end, as someone won't be with her.

They'll then hike into Rekavík Inlet, and from there along the rocky crest of Tröllakambur, where a polar bear was killed in 1917. The track is certainly rather tricky in places, so not the best of situations for those afraid of heights. And then she'll have to wade across the Höfn River estuary before tackling the mountain on the eastern side. She won't have a problem with that, she's very accustomed to it and is wearing all the right gear.

Somewhere she'll have to make herself some coffee. Take out her little Primus and boil some water, even pour it through a funnel. And someone will make a comment about that.

There's a fabulous view from the Kýrskarð Pass over Hornvík Inlet and down to Látravík, where the famous lighthouse stands. A phallic symbol on the edge of a cliff. A magnificent, historically famous place to stay, and one of the country's best-known lighthouse keepers, a renowned bookworm, lived there for a long time. She'll take a photo of the lighthouse and maybe get someone in the group to take a photo of her standing next to it.

Text message, 23:13: "Arrived in Látravík. Weather fabulous. Great beauty everywhere. Eating fresh Drangsnes haddock. Say hello to kids for me."

Hopefully she'll soon lie down to sleep in the lighthouse living quarters. Wonder if anyone will snore. Maybe someone will keep a promise to read out loud to everyone before sleep; the historian had sent enough material. Never know, somebody might read out something about the haunting of Hornvík, say something about the mutilated cow, for example, or mention the egg hunter who climbed Hornbjarg Cliff in Wellington boots one evening, just for fun. Good for those with a fear of heights to know about that, as is noted in one of the travel guides.

Then she'll do some soul-searching before sleep. Maybe take half an ibuprofen tablet to prevent stiffness in her hips the following day. And take a real hard look at herself, perhaps looking a bit sad.

July 13

SHE MUST HAVE SET OFF, it's already 10:00. They wouldn't have needed much time for morning chores today, because they're returning to the lighthouse in the evening. Yesterday the weatherman predicted banks of fog, and I wonder if it came ashore.

Somewhere along the way, the track becomes barely passable, but not enough to be dangerous. As the guide said at the preparatory meeting last winter, no one has frozen with fear there yet, though a few years ago, a woman did slide off the track down to a grassy field below.

Text message, 13:45: "Sitting on Kálfatindur peak, sun and clear skies. Tho fog creeping in along cliffs below."

Furthermore, even though she's so far away from a quarrel, she can't escape thinking about the man she married. The other couples and, yes, the divorced women in the group remind her of him. And maybe he'll be with her more than just on last year's hike, when she never walked next to him and had little or no inclination to talk to him. Later on, she said she thought some people like being by themselves.

Then there's the question as to what her travel companions manage to get out of her. She's certainly careful about what she says and has taken care through the years not to speak bad about her husband, but maybe she's had to give some sort of explanation.

The weather woman on channel 2 forecasts bright sunshine in the Hornstrandir area tomorrow. Especially gorgeous summer weather, she says.

No text message tonight. The boy with two girls up in his room.

July 14

TEXT MESSAGE, 08:55: "Are setting off. Weather looks good. Remember to post comment on dad on Facebook."

She's always on the ball, wherever she is. Her stepfather would've been seventy today, but he died almost a year ago, after a long illness. She took care of him day and night, of course, the whole time. She thought a great deal about this and asked our daughter to post:

"Dad would have been seventy today. Through him I learned

about human life, its kindness and its unfairness. I hereby commemorate him and let good recollections warm my heart."

Attached to it should be the song "Unforgettable" as performed by Natalie and Nat King Cole.

She herself is unforgettable. Her drive, joy of life, thirst for knowledge, sensitivity, love of travel, foresight, care, sexual energy. Moods. Her moods . . . But she means well, can't bear to see anything wretched any less than her father did. Always giving people something, asking them to come to dinner, go for a walk, and God knows what else, but neither does she shrink from asking them for something if necessary. And people seem to want to do favors for her.

All the same, it still happened the way it did.

Today is one of the more difficult days. They follow the route from Látravík up onto Mount Axarfjall and from there along Bjarnarnes, Digranes, and then the Smiðjuvík Cliff down into Smiðjuvík Inlet, which some people say was the model for Hagalín's well-known novel. A man once lived there who lost two young wives in childbirth within a short space of time. No midwife within reach, and so sex was a matter of life and death. Then his sixteen-year-old daughter went and died of exposure between two farmsteads, and her brother brought her body home to the farm in Furufjörður.

Up from Smiðjuvík there is an eight-hundred-foot-high ridge to cross before reaching Barðsvík Inlet, and from there, spread out for all to see, is one of the steepest mountain passes of the Westfjords. This was where one of the geologist Thoroddsen's horses missed its footing and rolled down the mountainside, side packs and all, without suffering any injury. From the pass they'll see the cabins in Bolungarvík Inlet.

She'll get through this, no need to worry about that; on the contrary, maybe it's the husband who's worried about what she's thinking along the way. Will she take a good, long look at herself? Be critical about herself and her behavior? Not certain she will, she's never been much for making apologies these last decades. He's been the one with all the faults.

"What's there for us when I get back?" she had asked, nonetheless, before she left.

But maybe she'll just think about her stepdad today. Sentimental song, "Unforgettable." Amazingly beautiful, and sung by father and daughter.

July 15

TEXT MESSAGE, 11:35: "Looking down on Furufjörður to the left and down onto Þaralátursfjörður to the right. Good weather. Set off at 7 this morning."

She must be at Svartaskarð pass by now, finished crossing the impassable Bolungarvík, for it's possible to get across it if the ebb tide is at least halfway out. They've taken this into account. And now the journey is nearing its stopping place, Reykjarfjörður, where the plan is to sleep in a tent. I wonder if she'll still do it, now she's on her own.

A famous tragedy took place in Furufjörður in the early twentieth century that a doctor reported after his trip there in 1928. The inhabitants were very subdued when he turned up, so he consequently started investigating. It turned out that a farmer in the fjord had gotten his stepdaughter pregnant, and the child was killed at birth. The doctor's account implies that the farmer's wife was involved, though she probably didn't kill the infant herself.

People lose it in all ages.

It seems like this was an especially good trip that would have been fun to go on. Maybe she didn't have to quit, but at least she gave him a chance to think about things. She stood in the doorway a long time, but after all that happened and even though the trip was paid for, it wasn't happening as far as he was concerned.

He is still finding splashes.

And it won't be easy to heal the wounds after what was said. Actually, it's not certain there's any desire to do so. Something has to give. Something will give.

Although the events leading up to it took a long time, the straw that finally broke the camel's back came the day before leaving. They were perusing a Norwegian weather forecast for the days of travel. This predicted very cold weather for the latter part of the trip, temperatures as low as 39°F, and he had allowed himself to curse. This didn't go over well, and she lambasted him for making everything so dull and negative. She could never enjoy preparing for trips, because he always destroyed all the pleasure in it.

There was a lot of truth in that. Anxiety needed some form of release, and she couldn't be bothered to listen anymore. It seemed she was tired of being sympathetic. Living with an anxious man is like living with a patient, not least because anxiety is infectious. And she doesn't want to be infected. She wants to enjoy life. It became more obvious now that she was an orphan.

"I want to enjoy being with you the way others enjoy being with you," she once said. "And how do others enjoy being with me?" he asked. "They find you funny and bold. I just get the problems, the tiredness, the unhappiness, the anxiety."

He should have kept himself in check. Been manly.

"I want a husband who's energetic. Who I can turn to. Someone who's not always complaining."

She then went to dinner with some friends she made on a trip abroad earlier in the year, a trip he didn't go on. He did want to show his daughter some support, on the other hand, and turned up at her soccer match. After that, he went for a long walk and then went to bed. When she came home, after he had turned the lights off, he heard her say, "You would've enjoyed the victory." "Yes," he replied, nothing more. But then he felt how she tried to soothe him by touching him in the same way he often touched her.

In the morning she asked, "Aren't you going to talk to me?"

"I don't know, one always says the wrong thing," he replied.

"I don't want to go with you if you're going to be so uptight," she then said.

And that's when he snapped.

Ugly.

Repulsive.

Took him more than an hour to clean up the worst of it. And he was still doing so. Strawberry jam in the most unbelievable places.

She's been sending text messages all the same, though actually there weren't any this evening. Probably her turn to do the cooking. That won't be a problem for her.

And the kids haven't asked after her. When our son heard her message, he said, "Good to know she's not dead, then." They wouldn't ask after him either. Teenagers are selfish by nature.

July 16

THEIR LAST DAY OF HIKING. Today they should hike out onto Geirólfsgnúpur headland and then maybe down into Skjaldabjarnarvík Inlet. If they don't get any fog, there'll be a great view from there both up toward the glacier and across the fjord both to the north and the south.

She's probably started getting to know some of her traveling companions a little better by now. Always easy for her to get to know people. Doesn't let them get too close, though, for obvious reasons. Disturbing to think about what might have been said between them. The future will depend on it. Maybe the divorced wives have had an influence on her. And that could go either way.

How will our reunion be? Will she come home tomorrow?

Text message, 13:19: "We r in Skjaldabjarnarvík. Going well and weather fine but fog on Geirólfsgnúpur. Best."

He specially noted the last bit: "Best."

A lot would depend on whether they could work things out when she got back. Two weeks of the holiday was still left, and it would be awful if it went down the drain after a difficult winter.

Could she overcome her contempt? Could he hold back the cause? Or was it totally up to her to deal with it?

She'll go to the pool when they return. Could see exactly how she'd think that would be nice.

The last time she came to Reykjarfjörður, her father was on the trip. His last trip.

July 17

DEPARTURE DAY. Uncertain when the boat will come to fetch them, probably not until just before noon. They'll be very busy clearing up, taking down tents, getting their baggage down to the pier. There was a possibility they'd get their gear transported for a reasonable price, but if that doesn't work out, there'll be a lot of work at hand, for it's quite a way from the swimming pool in Reykjarfjörður to the pier. The arctic terns will be shrieking at them as much as they can, too. Unless their young are dead, for there's been little fry this year.

Then there's the boat trip south to Norðurfjörður. South to a fjord called North! And then the car ride to Reykjavík. Sure hope nothing happens to her on the way, not now.

Texted her: "R u coming home tonite? If so, when? Best."

He tried to call her, but she didn't answer. When he tried again a little later, her phone was outside the service area.

He spent the day painting the hall. Two coats of frosty white. The kids are always leaving dirty finger marks on the walls.

And then she called. Her voice cheerful as if nothing had happened. Was happy with the trip. People had got on well together. Didn't know when she would be setting off southward. They still had to sort out the luggage, and then some of them were thinking of going to the swimming pool at Krossnes. She'd let us know as soon as she was setting off.

At nine o'clock he finally heard her open the front door.

"Hello there," she said.

Translated by Julian M. D'Arcy

Three Parables

MAGNÚS SIGURÐSSON

1. Lego

I HAD BOUGHT A WELL-KNOWN POEM by Inger Christensen, the Danish avant-garde poetess, on Amazon. It arrived duly, after two-day shipping, in a box of Legos. On the front of the box was a picture of a frigate from the Spanish Armada—the invincible fleet—although it didn't stay afloat much longer than the unsinkable ship that set sail from Southampton in 1912. I shook the box and heard how the poem rattled inside. But when I opened it and fished out the instructions, they turned out to be in Chinese, the language of Li Po and To Fu, who never had the chance to visit Legoland. I emptied the contents of the box on my desk and tried to figure out some of the words. Luckily, they were in a language I could claim some understanding of.

The resilient and strong ones that capture the wind and never give way, those must be the sails, I thought to myself and put a few sturdy pieces to the side—"mother," "nature," "time," and others of similar nature. "And the heavy and cold ones must be the cannons," I murmured, immersed now in my project, and stacked up another small pile of pieces containing such words as "hatred," "despair," and "fear." "And here's the helm!" I declared triumphantly when I glimpsed the alpha and omega of all the pieces in the pile, the piece that creates, controls, and assembles all the others.

By now the construction of my poetry vessel was going swimmingly, and I had started humming the Spanish cry of war, *No me mates con tomates*, when it suddenly dawned on me: could it be just a coincidence that "lego" means "I read" in Latin?

And before I knew it, I had become a galley slave chained to the rowing bench of a Roman warship, pulling at the oars under the steady beat of the *hortator*. Which is where I still am, whiling away the laborious hours in the same way as before: by assembling words. Which reminds me:

The Latin verb *lego* is originally cobbled together from the Danish words for "play" and "well": *lege godt*.

2. The Brain

I REPEATEDLY DREAM that I'm doing some frivolous spending. I'm generally a thrifty person, but I don't seem to be able to hold on to money in my dreaming world, a dimension in which I'm over my head in debt, in fact, for I'm easily persuaded by any "special" offer. But this dream was different, because what was being offered was something I truly and badly need: a brand-new brain.

The brains on offer were available in all shapes and sizes. But only the best would do for a deep-dreaming shopaholic, so I walked straight to the most expensive one and announced clearly to the brain merchant, "I'll take this one, please!" The merchant scrutinized me with his quick bird eyes, obviously well versed in the science of phrenology. "I'm sorry," he finally said. "This brain can be purchased only by one specific customer." After which the merchant uttered the name of a person who, for a long time now, has been of considerable nuisance to me. When I declared with all the joy I could muster that I was that very man, the merchant only smiled politely. It was as if he'd already heard this claim too many times before.

"Might I perhaps interest the good sir in the newest version of Thomas Brainhard instead?" he asked, pointing out a resilient drudge of a brain that, according to the description on the tag, would ensure a steady income and a stable family life. But Brainhard didn't interest me, nor did any other brain available in the shop, floating around in that peculiar gravity of formaldehyde. I wanted the brain that was made only for me and nobody else but that I was denied purchase, no matter what.

In the end I had to be pushed out of the door, the bird-eyed merchant frantically repeating these haunting words: "I am now going to close it. I am now going to close it!"

3. The Little Black Barrel of Ice

"I SEE THAT YOU'RE FULL OF SELF-HATRED."
I was in the public baths, relaxing after a long run, and had closed my eyes. I automatically assumed the words were directed at me. In front of me was a middle-aged man. Through the rising steam I could glimpse his sagging male breasts floating on the water's surface. Underneath the two breast sacks protruded a D-shaped belly. I couldn't help but picture the man's torso from the side as the letter "B"—two bulges, the smaller one for the breasts and the bigger one for the belly.

To be honest, I'm not sure if my alleged self-hatred, as undistinguished as it is, deserves to be mentioned at all. But I guess it's one of the things I'm trying to escape when I run. It's true that I've experienced the "loneliness of the long-distance runner," as a well-known author once called the self-flagellations of jogging. Nevertheless, I did find it presumptuous of the man to speak so categorically.

"You're miles off," I started, in my usual parlance of distance and proximity, but I realized right away that the accusation had been directed not toward me but instead to the man who now entered the hot tub, huffing and puffing. More precisely, the words referred to the "cold tub," a new option for visitors at the baths—a little black barrel, barely big enough for one average person (large as they've become), bearing a close resemblance to the boiling pots of certain southern tribes with questionable dietary habits. Except the water in the barrel is close to freezing, for health benefits—the excruciating cold being what the B-shaped man was referring to, as the fellow now entering the hot tub had briefly ventured into the barrel.

"It's good for what ails you," the iceman said as he plunged into the tub with a sigh. This one looked more like an "O" than a "B." Waves of water rushed over the concrete banks as he leaned back and displaced his round body's volume, much like Archimedes before him, although without any watershed in the history of science this time.

I myself most resemble the letter "I" (the small "i," in fact, rather than the big one), so not a great deal of volume shifted as I silently stepped out of the hot tub a little later. The sound of the men's voices petered out as I walked into the columns of steam, rising S-shaped from the warm baths into the black winter sky like snakes from a snake charmer's wicker basket—from all the tubs, that is, except the little black barrel of ice.

Translated by Magnús Sigurðsson

The Horse in Greenland

EINAR MÁR GUÐMUNDSSON

A XEL THE PLUMBER and Grímur the digger work on site together until lunch. Grímur finishes his job, and they go round to Axel's place for coffee. Grímur the digger takes his shoes off and walks into the living room in his work coveralls. He sits on the sofa and puts his feet up on the coffee table. He is wearing dirty wool socks.

"Hey, I completely forgot to ask you," says Axel the plumber, "how was it in Greenland?"

"It was fine," says Grímur the digger.

"Plenty of the fair sex to be found?" asks Axel.

"Yeah, I had three alone just to begin with."

"What, are you serious? Three?"

Sólveig, Axel's wife, walks by the living room on her way to the kitchen. She doesn't pay attention to them, but Grímur the digger looks at her.

"Hey, what's it take to get some coffee around here, old woman?" asks Grímur.

Sólveig looks at him in astonishment and walks away. Then Grímur turns to Axel and says, "How can you be married to such a sour hag?"

Axel tilts his head from side to side. He has long since turned a deaf ear to Grímur the digger's digs.

"Three, you say? I don't believe it," says Axel.

"I said three just to begin with," Grímur replies, "but I stopped counting after two months. I saw one woman when I was at the airport in Kulusuk. We went out for a minute, up against a wall behind the shed. And what do you think happened?"

"No, that I don't know," says Axel.

"You wouldn't believe it, but a horse came and bit me in the ass," Grímur says.

Sólveig comes in with a tray of coffee and bread, which she places in front of them. She looks at Grímur, but just then Axel says, "No, now you're lying."

"Lie! No, why should I?"

Sólveig walks away.

"There are no horses in Greenland," says Axel.

"Oh, I see. Then it must have been a reindeer."

They finish the coffee, and Grímur the digger smokes five Winston cigarettes. They stand up, and Grímur exclaims, "God damn bitch of a heart, she doesn't like all this coffee."

Axel calls out, "Sólveig, we're leaving now. Bye!"

Either she doesn't answer or they don't hear what she said.

Grímur finishes digging the foundation. And so he goes elsewhere to dig with his digger. He pays Axel a visit one Sunday. But it isn't a good time.

Axel takes Grímur aside. "It's not a good time. We're on our way to church."

"Church! Do you go to church?" asks Grímur.

"Yes," says Axel. "Because of the confirmation preparations. Hildur is going to have to be confirmed."

"Does that mean I'm not getting any coffee?"

"No, not now. We're going to be late."

Grímur leaves. More than a year passes. He has not dropped by since, nor has he called. The other day, Steini the foreman saw him in Bónus. Steini is married to Axel's wife's sister. Grímur the digger now has a Thai wife and three kids.

"You haven't dropped in on Axel?" says Steini.

"No, there's no visiting that bunch," says Grímur. "They're always in church."

"Got yourself a wife?"

"Yes," replies Grímur, "I met her during the summer holidays."

"Where did you go?"

"I stopped by Thailand."

"How was it there?"

"Fantastic."

"How does Thailand compare with Greenland?" asks Steini.

"It's impossible to put them in the same boat," says Grímur. "Greenland is like a convent compared to Thailand."

"And is everything going well?"

"Yes, very well," says Grímur. "Just a few language hitches, but we're both taking classes. She's learning Icelandic, and I'm learning English."

"Great."

"It's really no problem at all. I just lay my shirts on the table. When I come back, the buttons are all sewn back on."

So it goes for some time. Then I meet Axel the plumber at the community festival in Grafavogur, where fireworks are being set off.

"What's new with Grímur the digger?" I ask after a little chat.

"Oh, just the same as usual," says Axel. "He's divorced and bankrupt."

Translated by Alda Kravec

Laundry Day

ÁGÚST BORGÞÓR SVERRISSON

T HE WASHER WAS FULL OF SHIRTS AND BLOUSES, tossed in
with some undershirts. Óskar hung the shirts and blouses on
hangers in a row on the clothesline. Then it dawned on him that
Sigrún would prefer that he use clothespins to hang the clothes on
the line—but only after carefully smoothing out all the wrinkles.
She said that otherwise they'd wrinkle on the hangers and need to
be ironed twice. He asked why the hangers were there in the first
place, then, and she answered that they were for sweaters. But there
weren't any sweaters in the machine. That's nonsense, he thought,
the hangers don't crease my shirts, and he decided to ignore her. In
the beginning, she'd had to teach him how to do all of the housework, but now her gripes seemed arbitrary. For example, when he
vacuumed, she always snapped at him if he didn't immediately put
the vacuum back in the broom closet. But when she vacuumed—
and he admitted that she did it much more often than he did—the
vacuum cleaner sat in the middle of the floor for hours, even days
sometimes. If he said something about it later, she'd say she had
something left to do—vacuum behind the sofa, in the living-room
cupboard, or in the fridge—something so incredibly tedious that
he would've never thought to do it.

When they first got together, a quarter of a century ago, he
lived in an apartment that was piled high with beer cans and

cigarette butts. But since then a lot of water had flowed under the bridge, and it was as if she couldn't accept that he was fully capable of doing housework without a babysitter, as if she were struggling to have control over something. He sometimes toyed with the idea of going off on his own, hanging up only his own laundry, the way that he wanted, never putting the vacuum back in the closet. But of course he would never leave her. That was unthinkable, not because of the kids, they were already grown up, but because of all the other things. How would they explain it to the people who believed they had a perfect marriage (which it was, perhaps, after all; nobody believed that a perfect marriage was endlessly exciting)? How could they bear all of the talk around town? And if he lived in that apartment alone, it would probably get filled up again with empty beer cans, since nobody would be keeping track of what he drank, and he'd be left completely to his own devices. Nobody on earth cares if a man living alone in a rented apartment drinks a lot of beer in his own home. Inactivity would take over if he had no supervision, and then there was the task of buying himself a washing machine, bringing it into the laundry room, and hooking it up. He might be tempted to go to the laundromat, stick a coin in the machine, and sit and wait with a magazine or a book in his hands. He walked past a place like that the other day and could hardly think of a more depressing sight.

When he was finished hanging up all of the clothes from the laundry machine, he took Sigrún's blouses off the hangers and fastened them to the line with clothespins, just as she wanted. They were, after all, her clothes.

He was going to tidy up the bathroom before she came home, and he was going to use those moist, disposable wipes that she said were not strong enough to kill the bacteria around the toilet. It was all complete nonsense, as though she would always choose the method that was the most complicated and slow, as if there were more virtue in a difficult task than in a simpler and more efficient approach.

He switched off the light in the laundry room and went halfway up the dimly lit stairs. His thoughts about the many years before went out with the light.

....

He started, instead, to think about Thora, his younger brother Bragi's former live-in girlfriend from back in the nineties. The thought seemed unwarranted at first, but the reason for it gradually became apparent. Thora was a modest girl, not chatty, neither pretty nor plain. She carried out the housework with diligence and precision, even ironing underwear and tablecloths. She generally refrained from conversations at family gatherings, sometimes with the familiar chorus "Oh, I can't stand politics," even though the discussion had nothing to do with politics. Oskar was pleasantly surprised when he heard that Bragi had ended things with her. Thought that everything had gone so brilliantly; their daughter, Alma, had really flourished and they both worked hard, but they were free from financial difficulties. Thora was admittedly sick and tired of the brawls that Bragi ended up in when they went out to have fun. It was frustrating to have to go with her bloodied husband to the emergency clinic in the middle of the night or to watch the bouncer subdue him, wriggling on the floor, and an officer lead him out to a police car, all of this after looking forward all week to going to the basement of the National Theater to dance and after going to all the trouble of arranging a babysitter. One time, they had to pay a fortune for dental surgery for the man who had made the mistake of nudging Bragi in the bar. Bragi didn't consider himself a tough guy, but he didn't let anyone walk on him, and was unlucky enough that people who wanted to do so were constantly in his way.

These scenes didn't cause Bragi and Thora's separation. But when Thora ascertained that Bragi was beginning to entertain thoughts about a twentysomething girl, she kicked him out of the apartment. Threw his clothes out the window onto the sidewalk, where they landed like newly felled trees at a work site. Bragi had to gather them all up and stuff them into the backseat of the old Mazda while Thora rained down curses upon him from the window. A few days later, when she wasn't home, Bragi came back and carried more of his things out to a delivery van.

"I'm not ready to be buried alive, not in my thirties," he said to Óskar when the brothers met a few days later and it sounded like divorce was on his mind. They sat down with mugs of beer in one of the quieter pubs in town and spoke in low voices. Bragi said he had already decided to leave Thora long before he met that girl. The little adventure was over, it hadn't been anything, anything at all; he had just fled from the loveless Thora into some girl's arms.

"I can face reality. Life is sometimes porridge and boiled haddock, not an endless party, but to be with a woman who isn't in the mood to talk to you when you come home from work in the evening, who just carries on endlessly about dusting the apartment and watering the potted plants like some dumb machine, she never even bothers to go out, never, not to the pub or the movies, just sits at home all evening sulking, the clean freak. And the sex! My lord! Don't get me started on that."

"But this twenty-something girl, she's a total babe?"

"That's beside the point. She really doesn't matter."

"But do you have a picture of her or something? What's her name?"

Bragi shook his head and waved his hand. "Women never give you a break," he said and sighed deeply. He didn't say another word about it. A few years before, Óskar didn't find anything more tempting than a beautiful twenty-year-old girl. Now he considered them too young.

Bragi had stayed with his mother for the past few weeks, even though he'd also rented a flat in the city center. Stories began to spread, because Thora frequently visited there. Bragi's car was also spotted outside his former home. His mother beamed at this news, since she had always looked on divorce with disgust and figured

Thora a good match. When Bragi asked his mother to watch little Alma almost every week because her parents were meeting up, she believed she'd got it all worked out.

But now they had to wait for Bragi to go home to Thora. Óskar got curious and decided to call him up and ask about it.

"No, thank you! I'm not interested in going back to jail," Bragi scoffed.

Many years later, he would have to sit in an actual prison. But that's another story.

Years passed, one-two-three. Bragi and Thora split up, Bragi took up with other women, but he lived with them only for a little while before leaving. Sometimes he just had girlfriends. In any case, Óskar received reports that Bragi and Thora were once again giving it a shot. Gradually, Óskar lost interest. It was like listening to a broken record. Then he heard that Thora had finally left Bragi for another man, and with that it seemed that the long-drawn-out courtship was finally done with. A long while later, Óskar heard that Bragi had attacked Thora's partner. The first reports of this came from his mother, who was a notoriously unreliable narrator.

"Bragi and Thormar probably had a fight," she said into the phone. "I just wanted to let you know in case you hear something around town."

"Who's Thormar?"

"Thora's boyfriend!"

"Why'd they get in a fight?"

"I don't know, Thormar's not just dying of jealously, he's terrified for his Thora."

"So he went after Bragi?"

"Yes, exactly. His dad was some notorious brawler out west."

"But Bragi and Thora ended things years ago. Why would this Thormar be jealous?"

"Don't ask me. Bragi dropped in yesterday evening, and he had this awful neck sprain and was still after the guy, even though he could barely move his head."

"Where'd they fight? Any place in particular?"

"No, just Thora's house."

"And what was Bragi doing there? Isn't that a little strange, since it's been seven years since he flew the coop?"

"I don't know. He did have Alma with her. It might have something to do with his relationship with her."

This conversation stirred up more questions than it answered, so Óskar called his older sister, Bára, who had a closer relationship with Bragi than he did.

"It was all about the laundry. Thormar dared to have an opinion about Thora's washing Bragi's things."

"Was *Thora* washing *Bragi's* things? After all these years? Why on earth?"

"Well, Bragi doesn't have a dryer, neither does Mom, and he was sort of unhappy with how Lovisa hangs the clothes up and irons them."

"Who's Lovisa?"

"Bragi's partner. Haven't you met her?"

"I've never met her. I've never even heard of her."

"She moved in with him in autumn. An extremely good woman, but an awful kid, just twenty-two years old. And maybe didn't go to Home Ec in school, like Thora did, you know how she is."

"Why can't he just hang up his own things? And iron them?"

"That's what Thormar took issue with."

"Yeah, but why? I've been hanging up and ironing my own laundry for a lot of years, and I have a girlfriend. What's wrong with this guy? And her, for that matter?"

"It's this terrible codependency, that horrible disease I know all too well myself and I really need to recover from."

Óskar sighed. Bára had left years before, and after the divorce, she testified about her ex-husband's drinking and psychological abuse. Óskar sympathized with her but had become tired of the way she handled all the strange and undesirable behaviors of people with that disease. She was eternally calling people patients, terminally ill, so that one imagined them lying unconscious in a hospital room, with countless tubes plugged into a just-barely-alive body, when in reality the person was filled with vitality, pressing on and wrangling with the havoc and chaos that only truly healthy people could cause.

....

The fight happened in Thora and Thormar's laundry room. Bragi went there to fetch his laundry and iron his shirts, towels, underwear, tops, and jeans; everything was ready to go and stacked neatly in two laundry bags in front of the dryer. The ironing board was lying open beside them, the iron sitting on top.

That day Thora really laid into him with previously unstated objections to his laundering. He didn't listen to them, just strode busily past her to his clothes, waving "hey, hey," as soon as the front door opened (he had opened it with a key until Thormar moved in after they bought Bragi out; so they changed up the locks, and Bragi had to adjust without saying a word about the switch, which is to say, he rang the bell and strode in once the door was opened). But Thora continued. She was saying something to him that he didn't hear, because he was thinking distractedly about a meeting he was anticipating—he was going to meet a man in about an hour to talk business over a cup of coffee, but before he could do that, he had to take his clothes home and tell Lovisa to put them in the closet.

He was down in the laundry room and had been sitting there contentedly on his haunches for a little while, surrounded by the scent of his freshly pressed and laundered clothes, when he finally heard Thora talking. He heard her shout, "You hear that, Bragi? This can't go on any longer!"

He looked up from the canvas bags, where everything was as it should be, and in the next thirty to sixty seconds, his satisfaction turned into burning rage.

Thora stood in the doorway of the laundry room, her fists on her hips (the way women sometimes do when trying to seem determined), but she looked at him with dread. He caught a glimpse of Thormar behind her, and that was when he realized that Thora had been jabbering at him for a few minutes and her jabbering had gotten muddled with Thormar's jabbering.

Óskar rose slowly to his feet, appraised his situation, and let silence fill the laundry room for a good, solid minute until he said, "Are you his dummy, woman? If he has something to say to me, can't he say it directly to me?"

Thormar stepped out from behind Thora, slipped his fingers into his belt loops, and stood in a solid straddle in front of Bragi. But he looked frightened. He was rather small in stature, like Bragi, but not in build—he had a little potbelly—and was just about thirty years old but with beautiful, wavy blond hair, blue eyes, and a face that probably made women swoon.

"We won't put up with this laundry circus any longer. . . . It's like . . . it's like some free dry cleaner." His voice faltered.

Bragi glared at this man—he had succeeded so well at swallowing all of his jealousy up to that point. Had just suffered in silence and given no indication that he was displeased with this stranger, this bastard who slept with Thora, the girl that Bragi imagined would always, in some sense, reside in his bones.

I never let anyone carry me. And this is the thanks I get!

Now his long-bottled-up jealousy came out, and he laid out his resentment on this busybody who would destroy the perfect laundry arrangement and the good and normal friendship of this formerly cohabitating couple. His fist and forearm, which seemed to shoot out from him, were fueled by an anger that was both old and new and a power that was so big that Bragi had to soften the blow before it landed, but not before Thormar hurtled backward, crashed into the wall, and slid down it like a saloon fighter in those old westerns.

"HAVE YOU NEVER DONE YOUR FRIENDS A FAVOR, YOU
DUMB FUCK!" Bragi screamed at him. Thormar wiped blood from
his nose and probed his split lip with his fingers. But then he
suddenly pummeled Bragi, quick as lightning, with unexpected
tenacity; they stumbled as if in a slow and drawn-out dance, like
astronauts on the moon, except each had the other in a headlock
(hence the neck sprain Bragi complained about to his mom),
neither able to pin the other, and neither about to release his grip
until Thora threatened to call the police.

....

It may well be true that Sigrún tidied up more often than he,
but she still has to admit that he has gotten a lot better about it. If
she, for example, goes on a trip without him, he sees to it that, more
often than not, everything is clean when she comes back. So let's
not forget that he takes care of the car and sundry maintenance
issues that arise from time to time. Now he flashes forward to Sigrún getting back from the cottage, where she's spent the weekend
with her friends. He's in a great mood after cleaning the bathroom,
where he liberally used the disposable wipes, contrary to Sigrún's
recommendation, and vacuumed and scrubbed all the floors with
a damp mop. He decides to leave the vacuum in the middle of the
living-room floor. She wouldn't dare wag her finger at him after
all of the pains he's taken! But then he thinks that there's honestly
no reason to spoil this perfect picture, and he pushes it into the
cleaning closet.

He wonders whether she'll be in the mood when she gets
home that evening. After all, he wouldn't spoil this immaculate
sight for nothing; she could certainly be in a good mood after a
successful weekend with her friends.

But it was just as likely that she'd say she was too tired when
he tried to feel her up in bed; she'd kiss him on the cheek, say
good night, and roll over. He'd be frustrated but decide not to say

anything; instead, he'd get out of bed and down three or four beers, maybe a shot, too, maybe two, actually, maybe drink as much as he could as quick as he could without getting drunk as such. She'd know what he was doing, but she wouldn't say a thing about it, she'd just let the silent resentment soak into her dreams along with the stink of booze and the feeling that it's maybe just some people's lot in life to be continually disappointed in one other.

Translated by Megan Alyssa Matich

Scorn Pole

ÞÓRARINN ELDJÁRN

W E FINISHED BUILDING THE TURF HOUSE at Skörð at
seven minutes past five on Sunday evening. It was within
an hour of our planned completion, but with barely one and a half
days to spare before our final deadline: shooting was starting first
thing Monday morning.

The final heave had been tough, an unceasing drudgery lasting
more than a fortnight, and so we felt great lying there on the earth
at tools-down, letting fatigue seep from our bodies. We opened the
bubbly, fished ice-cold from the stream, and sipped it by turn from
the plastic glasses our master builder, Kjartan, had bought at the
store in Helvík.

The weather couldn't have been more glorious: not a cloud
scratching the heavens; dead calm. We lay there shirtless and in
shorts as the late June sun did for our outer stress what the sparkling wine did for our inner fatigue: a bubbling sense of well-being
fizzed in every atom within us, a ticklish pleasure for both mind
and body.

But the greatest sense of satisfaction belonged, as it should, to
our pride in the creation itself, the turf house of Björn in Skörð.
It shone in the sun, its four gables with ornamental carving, a
gleaming prow jutting into the farmyard, a fresh green roof of turf
squares so beautifully cut and masterfully fit together that no one

could see a single flaw. And on the sides and at the back, brilliantly and painstakingly assembled rock pilings on the walls and herringbone walls that showed all the tricks of the trade. "A real treat for the lens," the Dutch director of photography said, beaming with satisfaction and eager anticipation when he came by for a brief field visit.

....

We had cut all the turf after studying ancient methods, quarrying stones from far and wide and cutting them to the exact size, sliced snug into the walls. The master, Kjartan, had watched over everything, a man with his mind in the past, passionate about bygone methods. Nothing could be imperfect; he put all his efforts into his work, and his zeal and professionalism infected the rest of us.

We were sure that this wasn't just some turf shack to be used only as a kind of scenery. No, this was the turf house of Björn in Skörð, and all the crucial scenes in the movie would take place around the farm, all about it, and especially inside it—as should be no surprise to someone who knew Steindór Vatnsness's acclaimed novel.

The evening was young, and within each of us brimmed an unfamiliar, seductive feeling of promise. Master Kjartan was awaiting his wife and children, due to arrive from the south with their caravan for the weekend. He couldn't wait and was constantly asking our opinion as to how he should best go about strengthening the suspension on the caravan so it would last through the first night. The carpenter, Steingrímur, his buddy, was going to drive into town and visit his sweetheart and newborn daughter. And so he was going to dip only the tip of his tongue into our champagne, just for solidarity. But there was something of the lush about him, as his friend Kjartan used to say: he had great difficulty leaving his tongue to get refreshment alone. His lips constantly found themselves in the fluid, and then his throat would want a turn, too.

Þrándur and I also had plans for an exciting visit. It so happened that Guðrún and Rósa, our friends from school, were working in a summer hotel in the neighboring region. They had some time off and a car and were planning to come see us; we were all going to go dancing in Helvík. Þrándur and Guðrún were going steady, and I was full of plans to make sure that evening would see Rósa and me getting together. It was time to put an end to all the awkwardness. The preceding months my whole game had been totally solid, and through Þrándur I knew that the ground was prepared. Nothing left except the final heave. I was totally certain that this evening it was going to happen.

Master Kjartan slapped the cassette in the machine. The turf house glowed in the evening sun, and once again the sound of the Beach Boys resounded over the fields: "Good Vibrations." Master Kjartan had two passions in life. Apart from the history, building methods, and construction techniques of Icelandic turf houses, the Beach Boys occupied his every thought. He was a walking encyclopedia when it came to their songs and career; he rattled off facts and anecdotes time out of mind. In the middle of a lecture on turfs and wedge walls and turf cutting, he would set out on a long speech about the Wilson family and Mike Love in California. Hörður Ágústsson, the Icelandic artist and turf-house scholar, and Brian Wilson: they were his guys.

Þrándur and I initially found them mildly amusing, these much-admired surfer hippies who seemed to have been made up from somewhere in Kjartan's young years, but the master never yielded ground, and after many weeks of his zealous missionary work, we felt the same way. We had become their faithful admirers. At every opportunity we lustily took up the tunes' refrains, and even Steingrímur could not bear to be left out of our four-voiced falsetto accompaniment of the virtuoso Brian and his talentless brothers and cousin: "I'm picking up good vibrations."

And then everything really was vibrating: we were, inside and out, the farm was, and the mountains in our eyesight, and suddenly the earth itself, too. Or was this an earthquake? We looked at each other, Kjartan shut off the cassette player, and we rose to our feet. We immediately saw what had caused everything to shake: an oversized jeep clambering up the drive from the highway to where it now stood in the hay meadow. Master Kjartan squinted his eyes curiously in the direction of the vehicle, and then a broad smile moved across his countenance.

"And look what we have here! A distinguished visitor!"

"Royalty?" asked Steingrímur, taking off his glasses.

"Even better. Approaching us is none other than the district magistrate himself, come to check out our handiwork. What do you say about that, lads?"

He was glowing. Nothing seemed to excite master Kjartan more than getting to show influential people his craft, being given permission to expound on his methods and theories and to absorb the resulting praise and compliments for his professionalism and industry. He was so joyous and happy that he acted as though he didn't hear Steingrímur's remark: "Unless he's come to issue a prohibition order."

The car door opened, and it was indeed the area magistrate, Ásgeir Fertramsson, who stepped out from the driver's side; from the rear door came none other than Sigurjón Már Sigurjónsson, the movie's director and producer. They got down from the car, opened the trunk, and took out a massive cardboard box, which they carried between them across the field.

Amazed, we watched their journey. The movie company had originally had a fair few quarrels with the magistrate, no doubt involving all kinds of arguments and demands about getting permission for the movie's assorted filming requests. The saying was that you couldn't even drive a nail into the wall somewhere in the district without the magistrate's having to interfere in some way. People in the magistrate's administrative district were generally said to be extremely afraid of him, and, moreover, he had this mean trick of liberating people from their driver's licenses whenever they annoyed him. Kjartan giggled with pleasure and looked at us.

"It's flabbergasting that little Siggy here managed to lick the temper out of the bastard, even getting him to run petty errands with him!"

The passenger-side door opened, and an old geezer appeared in the doorway. He clambered slowly and awkwardly down from the tall jeep, but then briskly caught up with his fellow travelers, supported by a staff.

The newcomers stepped into the farmyard and set the cardboard box down, greeting us. Sigurjón Már seized everyone by the hand and shook heartily, including Þrándur and me. It was part of his directorial style that everyone who worked on the film was equally important. He placed great store in being rousing and encouraging; all those who worked with him were variously geniuses, heroes, or champions.

"Greetings, virtuosi! Just finished? But of course! You're men after my own mind! We've brought with us the prop, the scorn pole," he said, pointing to the cardboard box.

Next, he introduced us to the lawman. The magistrate was most amiable, looking everywhere in a friendly way, and didn't seem to be on the lookout for our driver's licenses, at least for the moment. The owl-like old man who was with them seemed, by contrast, not the least concerned with our presence. Instead, he waddled in a bowlegged fashion straight toward the turf house. He was very old, with a stern expression; he had horn-rimmed glasses and a flat cap. He wore a dark blue, double-breasted pinstripe jacket, which glistened with age, and grayish baggy pants, just as old and from a completely different suit. He also had on a darkish shirt, its collar fraying, and a yellowed tie around his neck. On his feet were gray and red thick wool socks and old brown athletic sandals.

We watched the guy, taken aback. He'd started snooping into all the nooks of the turf house, fingering the piled rocks and the turfs, prodding the divet strips along the walls, and muttering things to himself—and then he disappeared inside.

"This really is something for my old man," the magistrate said, half apologetic. "He was born in a turf house, and so by nature he is rather immersed in the old ways."

"Yes, it's a windfall for an old man, naturally," said Sigurjón Már, and then the magistrate and he continued to chat pleasantly, comparing now and then, uttering all the old phrases about how that generation had made the jump directly from medieval times into the modern era. He'd been born into the crafts and know-how of the ancient Age of Settlement, but now sat and watched television and wrote at electric typewriters and even computers. I found it hard to imagine this old man in front of a television, and I thought he might sincerely agree with the Beach Boys when they sang, "I just wasn't made for these times."

I noticed that master Kjartan did not pay much attention to this chatter; it was like he was constantly trying to lead the conversation somewhere else. Clearly he was, as ever, beside himself at getting a chance to show such powerful men the turf house, but perhaps there was also somewhere inside him some disquiet as to what this owlish old man was messing about with inside the house. Finally he couldn't stand the situation a moment longer, and broke somewhat gruffly into the good-natured chat right in the middle of one of the magistrate's sentences:

"Indeed, but I think it's now high time we get to show you our masterwork. There's no small amount of care and diligence put into it. And, truth be told, I think that our lawman here might decide for himself whether there isn't a lasting value, a chance to discuss the possibility of using this structure to strengthen tourism in the region. I have no doubt at all that after the movie has had its big success, it will become popular and sought-after to visit and even to stay overnight at the farm of Björn in Skörð.

Sigurjón Már evidently understood where the wind was blowing. As soon as we all began to move slowly toward the farmhouse,

Kjartan was forging ahead with his customary lecture, telling stories of Icelandic architecture in nutshell. He described the woven external structure of the turf house, the major methods and terminology, and his own insights and ways of working. Sigurjón Már regularly interjected words of admiration and repeatedly made it known that Kjartan was a major specialist in this area, a hero, champion, and virtuoso. No lie, Kjartan. That's what we'd expect from someone of our caliber. It goes without saying. Their interplay was admirable. The magistrate listened closely and seemed dutifully interested—keen, even. Kjartan played up to this reception and was soon getting lyrical and highfalutin, not least because the bubbles hadn't entirely escaped out of him yet.

We, his coworkers, were also filled with pride, enchanted. To this point, it had only been a preface, but now it was time to go inside the turf house. Master Kjartan pushed the door from the hinge, came to a halt outside, and gestured the guests in with respectful waves of his hand, bowing his head to each as he said, "No, my pleasure, after you."

Yet they never got to enter. At the very same moment that Ásgeir the magistrate was lifting his heel over the threshold step, he collided with Fertram, his father, who came bustling out with long strides, ripping off his glasses and waving them high in the air with his other hand in order to punctuate his words. He had become cross-eyed with agitation, turning up his nose and complaining.

"Uhhhhh, a crying shame! Never in all my life have I seen such meddling. What's here is literally nothing like what it's supposed to be. Nothing like it actually *was*!"

I saw master Kjartan wilt and take a step backward. He didn't speak, not out of composure but because he was simply unable to speak, so upset was he. The magistrate became ill at ease, looking at the rest of us with a wretched, puckered smirk of nervousness that seemed apologetic. He began at once to try to calm the man.

"You shouldn't always be so harsh, father. You need to remember that these poor boys have tried to do it as well as they can."

"I'm well aware of that," replied the old man. "As well as they can, definitely. I don't doubt it a moment. The problem is exactly that: they clearly can't do anything. These impossible fops who claim to be a match for the job and say they know but who couldn't find their butt cheek with their right hand. Nor any place else!"

He raised his staff and lashed out at one of the walls, the very one Kjartan had taken such great pains with, the very one the Dutchman had adored for its cinematic beauty.

"See this here, for example, is this what they're calling a wedge wall? It's wedged in there all right, this heap, you could say so. The peat is cut lopsided, dried all wrong, and no one ever put one together like it. And the divet strip—if you could even call it a strip—is nothing but a lump of mud."

"Calm down, father, you shouldn't get all worked up about it. You know it's not good for you. I think you are being too harsh a judge. Isn't it praiseworthy when young men show enterprise, when they seek out the old ways and get interested in them?"

"Oh, is that so? That's how it is when one learns only from books: these days there's a thirst for everything old, provided it's not old people. They could go out and ask aged and learned men, but in all likelihood they're far too smug to do that."

He turned on his heel and swept away in the direction of the car. The magistrate looked at us, embarrassed, but when he saw the expression on Kjartan's face, his blood ran quick to duty and he resolved to go help his father.

"As I said, he was raised in a turf house, and . . ."

And then he turned away and skulked after the man, as though he was scared he would run into some danger, or might drive off alone in a temper in that colossal jeep. Master Kjartan was now finally able to address the matter, and called after the magistrate:

"Raised in a turf house, yes, but in the seventeenth century? That's a seventeenth-century farmhouse, tell him that I could tell you, according to Hörður Ágústsson . . ."

He didn't continue. Sigurjón Már had come all the way up

to him and stood on his foot, a forceful indication he should say nothing more.

Then, in a quiet voice, through clenched teeth, he said, "Calm down, man, don't you go and destroy everything I've worked at in order to get in good with this worm of a magistrate. What matters the jabbering of an old imbecile?"

The director sauntered away in the direction of the father and son, who had by now reached the jeep; he turned back to us once to signal that we should keep calm—and not without good reason, since we had to hold Kjartan back or he would have steamed after them. We didn't let him go until the jeep had turned away from us and set off down the slope.

With that, we were free. But it was soon clear as day that all the wonderful energy that prevailed had now evaporated after the visit. The tingling sensation, the sense of expectation: vanished. The vibrations in the air were no longer good. Even the weather took part: clouds drew across the sun, and in no time at all a strong wind whipped up.

Kjartan was very evidently far past anger. He gripped a shovel and brought it to bear by turns on tussocks in the farmyard and said he was imagining flogging the behind of the old bastard who had destroyed our day—and of the wormy magistrate his son, too. The day? He'd destroyed half a month's toil, destroyed our entire satisfaction from a well-done job. We fell headlong over one another competing to tear strips off this elderly figure.

"Damned old-timey brag-asses, thinking they always know better than everyone else, that they're some kind of specialist simply because they were born before the turn of the century," said Kjartan. "It's this sort of person who thinks things are beyond the pale if they aren't done exactly the way they once were, entirely accidentally, in the particular hellish dog mound where they were born and where their dismal life started."

We each and every one made our contribution: tried to curse the man as harshly as possible, to mimic him, going about bowlegged and coiling our fingers around our eyes to signal glasses.

"And what's that about reaching our hands to grab our asses?" asked Þrándur. "Why should we? Reckon he is queer on top of everything else?"

Things escalated from there as we tried to outdo each other, insulting and faulting the man. His ears needed to be burning feverishly in that jeep.

Suddenly a bottle of vodka came into play in place of the champagne. Somehow it magically appeared from Steingrímur's bag. The bottle passed resonantly among us and was finished fast and madly, and another came in its place. We were all dead drunk in an instant, so hungry and fervid were we. And we took a solemn oath that something needed doing to punish the man. Steingrímur wanted us to attack him, to chase down the threesome and thrash the evildoer. Þrándur joined in, and they eagerly dared us to come along and get in the car with them. The motion failed, though, because Kjartan and I felt that, despite everything, it wasn't a good idea or a strong plan to get into a car blind drunk in order to assault the aged father of the local magistrate.

"Scorn pole," screeched Kjartan, pointing to the cardboard box that Sigurjón Már and the magistrate had left behind at the farmyard. "We'll raise a scorn pole against him; that will teach him a lesson."

The plan was well received. We staggered over to the box, opened it, and drew out of it the raw materials for a scorn pole, a sorcerous, looming rod wrapped around with a mess of seaweed and rotting wool fragments and featuring a rather fearsome horse head. The props department had carried out some excellent work spinning this up: it seemed to have half-rotten skin and flesh around a horse skull, truly gruesome, with totally yellow teeth and burst plastic eyes. It was missing nothing except for the smell and the larvae and the flies. It all seemed real.

We drove the pole into the earth on a hill directly east of the turf house and flung the head on the stick so that it faced in the direction of Helvík, reckoning that's where the man was headed. Then we started a kind of ceremony we cooked up on the spot, fashioned from knowledge Þrándur and I had learned from *Egil's Saga* the past winter and from some pretty savage stuff we'd seen on television, and spiced up with bits of popular occultism from Kjartan and Steingrímur. We stomped around the pole in a war dance of sorts, getting all the more wild the less was left in the vodka bottle. Kjartan pulled together an invocation, some doggerel we recited and chanted time and again in order to direct the libel all the better against the old man:

> *O be fearful, angry bully!*
> *O witless Fertram!*
> *We taunt you, dog,*
> *fodder for our fun.*
> *Let fate hide Fertram*
> *in Hell's thievst grip.*
> *Let his family feel taunted,*
> *The cross-eyed pinworm.*

It was nothing short of amazing that this rigmarole should stick with me despite everything being so chaotic, individual moments falling away and blurring into a single picture. We danced the dance constantly, by now practically naked. We set a fire under the scorn pole and took it in turns to piss on the flames. People were constantly coming and going, there was uproar about this and that, for this reason or that reason—and then all went black.

I remembered it all rather hazily the next day, except for the verse, which thundered again and again, verbatim, in my head, resounding in time with the hammering blood of my hangover.

It was a subdued crew that started waking up, one after another, some way into the following day. We were proof of the old wisdom that says no one decides where he's going to sleep: accident seemed to have dictated that each slept where he was, in whatever position. With tremendous collective effort, we set ourselves to slowly piece together the previous evening and night. A mosaic gradually emerged, finally complete and yet not at all splendid:

Some time after the dance had reached its peak, Kjartan's wife showed up with her children and the caravan, only to drive off in a flurry when she saw the state of her husband. Not long after that, our girls arrived, Guðrún and Rósa. At that time we were nothing less than buck naked, pissed out of our skulls as we tried incessantly to pull them into the dance and to feverishly explain what was going on, that we were shouting destruction down on the idiot who had ruined the turf house for us, yes, who'd ruined our summer, yes, who'd ruined master Kjartan's whole life.

I saw it all before me in bright lights. Kjartan's weeping children as their mother led them away. Steingrímur gone completely nuts, so much so we needed to use force to stop him from driving away at once, out of his wits and raging drunk. And the worst thing of all: the incredulous, horrified expressions on the faces of Guðrún and Rósa before they drove off in terror and confusion.

"This is sick. You all are sick." That was the only thing they were able to stammer out.

And so the evening's infinite promise had crash-landed: Kjartan about to lose his family, and Þrándur no longer going steady; my glorious hope for Rósa and me come to nothing; Steingrímur shattered from his sweetheart and baby in town, and immobilized in Skörð, since we hadn't a clue where we'd put the car key. In all likelihood we'd thrown it somewhere amid the peaty tussocks. Steingrímur tried to spark the car by linking up the connections, but his hands were too shaky to get the wires together. And that devil of an old man was to blame for it all.

We weren't fit for any major undertaking but passed the day pulling ourselves back together. We needed to consider various things: clothes and work gear, bottles and plastic bags lay across the area like raw lumber. It all needed gathering up before the film crew came the next day. In one place the rocks had been taken down, which reminded us that Steingrímur had gone berserk, trying to noisily break everything until we took away his freedom of movement.

All that brouhaha served to give us some distraction until evening, when we'd all finally stopped puking and could start to think about simmering up a bite to eat for dinner. Most surprisingly, we were in a lively mood, even given everything. Kjartan bristled spiritedly and said it was immaterial, that there's no reason to care about such a man, and it was completely useless to worry about women in general. Under such circumstances, it would become clear what stuff they were made of. A wife who let such a trifle make her bolt from her man was worth nothing. I wasn't entirely sure the same thing applied to Rósa.

It was nearly time for the news, so our master turned on the radio, saying that it would do well to find out that somewhere in the world something more newsworthy might have happened than some craftsmen going on a binge.

The announcer was finishing up with a death notice, and we didn't pay any attention, but a deep and paralyzing silence calm came over our group when he started the next one. "Our father, Fertram Ásgeirsson, former farmer and district council chairman from Hóli, passed away yesterday evening in the nursing home in Helvík. Ásgeir Fertramsson, Guðbjörg Rósa Fertramsdóttir . . ."

We said nothing for a long time, just sat there with gaping maws, not sure what we should do, whether laugh or cry. None of us seemed to notice even that the main story on the evening news concerned a group of workers starting to tear down one of the oldest houses in town. Even Kjartan was stone silent. Finally Steingrímur broke the silence, and folded. He cried loudly and sobbed constantly:

"We have become murderers. I am a murderer. I am a murderer!"

It was at that moment we heard some thunder of a new machine. Someone was coming along the pathway. We startled badly when we saw who was on the way: none other than the magistrate.

"What the hell," said Kjartan, "your silly girlfriends must have told tales on us. Damn rich girls, damn highbrow pussies. Why on earth did you bring them here? But I won't deny it. Don't think that thought. Let's see what he's up to. He'll never get my driver's license from me, that much is sure."

The magistrate had made the trip unaccompanied and was getting out of the car. We were silent, waiting to see what he wanted. Steingrímur had stopped weeping. Kjartan noiselessly whistled "California Girls," his habit when occupied in a difficult task. He waited to see what would happen.

The magistrate came over to the farmyard and wished us a good evening. He acted like nothing had happened. There was no sense this was a man who had suddenly lost his father. Or that that he was standing now in front of us taunters, us outrage-men, planning to make an accusation against us.

"Greetings, all, and thanks for yesterday," he said, completely friendly.

I weighed for a moment whether it would be right to offer him condolences or something similar, but immediately felt it would just awaken suspicion.

"The old man left his glasses here yesterday; perhaps you've come across them?"

We said nothing, hungover and silent, too paralyzed to say anything. The magistrate looked loosely around him, then slipped into the turf house. He had no confidence in us. No feelings. But something was building, perhaps just the calm before the storm. As soon as the magistrate had gone, Kjartan rose to his feet and strolled calmly in the direction of the scorn pole and seemed to adjust it a bit. Probably he was making it look like we were right in the middle of working, but I felt it was careless of him to so brazenly draw attention to the crime scene, and to the murder weapon itself.

The magistrate immediately returned. He stopped a moment and regarded the scorn pole, where Kjartan was still fussing.

Then he said, "So, I see you've already fixed up the pole? It's sure to be a great scene. And it had better be, if it's to match the novel. Well, I didn't find his glasses. You hold on to them until later, and let me know if you discover them."

He went off toward the car. Once he'd got inside, started the engine, and set off, Kjartan took out the late Fertram's glasses, which he had suddenly remembered and managed to snag from the scorn pole in time. He looked after the magistrate through the dead man's thick glasses and crossed his eyes.

Steingrímur began weeping again. "Aren't you going too far? Why didn't you let the wretched guy have his glasses?"

"Wretched orphan!" mimicked master Kjartan. He took the glasses, folded them, and slipped them into his breast pocket.

"What do you think he'll need glasses for on the other side? He'd just start criticizing everything in hell, and get treated even worse as a result."

Then Kjartan took the car keys and flung them vigorously at his buddy. "Go on into town and stop being such a namby-pamby." He waved energetically in the direction of the road and started running down the slope.

A yellow car with a trailer behind it was moving cautiously up the pathway.

Translated by Lytton Smith

Harmonica Sonata in C Major

GUÐMUNDUR ANDRI THORSSON

GUNNAR ALWAYS REMEMBERS THE MORNING they had together as teenagers in downtown Reykjavík. They were on Amtmannsstígur at about five or six in the morning, and they came out of a party and walked up and down Thingholt as if they were lost—they weren't—down this street and that street and then another until they arrived at Amtmannsstígur again and stopped in their tracks as if they'd found a place that doesn't exist, a place where time doesn't exist. Gunnar always remembers that morning, although he won't speak about it to anyone. The morning sun bathed all the houses and gardens and cars, and he took his harmonica out of his pocket and said, "Wait, just wait, and listen," and started playing her a song. Without stopping, he said, in the middle of a draw, "Wait, just wait, this is for you." She stood stock-still and pigeon-toed and listened to him, tall and thin and serious, and tucked a lock of her hair behind her ear, and even though the weather was calm and she was wrapped in a parka—her green parka—she folded her arms as if it were a little cold. Meanwhile, the street was asleep—people in houses, birds on roofs, cats under cars. Suddenly he noticed a cat that'd just woken up and now stood in front of him staring accusingly, and so he finished the song with a buoyant glissando, placed the harmonica back in his pocket, pulled her into his chest, and she caressed his neck with her hands and they kissed in this secret place on Amtmannsstígur, the place that did not exist. It was a morning kiss. It was a night kiss. It was their first kiss and their last kiss, their best kiss, and their only kiss.

Even though they'd often kissed.

"How long were we together, again?" he says to her out of nowhere, and as he pours the coffee, he sees that she's stiffened up even though her back is turned to him. He immediately regrets the question. He's afraid it sounded too abrupt, too halfhearted, but he doesn't know how he could have softened it, he can't even approach her anymore—doesn't know anything about how she thinks. He concentrates on the coffee brewer, lets the boiling water reach all of the coffee in the funnel, as his father taught him—to do it all just right—and he discovers that the tip of his tongue is sticking out of the corner of his mouth, just as when he was a boy and was allowed to brew the coffee for his father to take out to him in the garage when he was not at sea and his father glanced up from his work, poured from the pot into his cup, and said, Wait, just wait, sipping and nodding his head meaningfully, and said, You've really made some progress here, Gunni boy. This morning, he looked at himself in the mirror and felt like he was eleven years old. But he's not eleven years old—he recently turned fifty, had a birthday party with a few friends and colleagues who celebrated how long he'd lived and what a truly good fellow he was. She wasn't there.

When he turns around, he sees she's looking out the window at Kata from the choir, who's riding a bicycle in a white dress with blue polka dots. She herself is wearing a blue sweater, as if it's cold outside despite the sun, and she probably finds it cold here after all those years abroad, but the neck of her sweater is wide, and he's staring at her collarbone. He looks at her hair that's no longer soft and wavy down to her lower back. It's short now, and it is dyed with a shade of dark brown that gives it a dry and worn appearance. She still has the same big nose—with the same small wrinkle in the middle of her forehead just like the line between two hemispheres, still the same thin, soft chin that he longs to stroke, the same blue eyes that can send him anyplace on earth.

She doesn't answer him. She doesn't say anything, just keeps staring at the woman on the bike, seeming almost perplexed. Maybe she doesn't quite remember it like he does and needs to think about it, and maybe she believes that he doesn't remember their four years, three months, five days, thirteen hours, and six minutes together. After they were teenagers.

Perhaps she feels he shouldn't stumble so clumsily into their sanctuary.

He doesn't know how she thinks.

....

Maybe she thinks things will never be the same. They found each other when they were teenagers and listened to music that her aunt in Reykjavík sent her from the record shop. And it was very important music. It was hard-core music, full of blasting guitar riffs and insalubrious synthesizers and angst. They sat in silence and concentrated on understanding these metallic, queasy harmonics arisen out of the gray big cities in England, where everyone was unemployed—here, there was enough work for everyone, as his father never tired of saying to his brother, who sometimes complained that there was *nothing* here. These thin, nasal voices that had been carried here to this village on the winds of civilization were oddly suited to the drizzly weather, biliousness, remoteness, and industriousness here. The record turned on the gramophone in his room like a seductive black hole, and they stared at it fixedly until it reached the last groove, hissed, and automatically clicked back into place, and they sometimes sat for a while and said nothing about themselves and their lives. His mom was in the kitchen, quietly tending to rags and reality, while his brother sat in his own room and repeatedly fired a sawed-off shotgun in one of his video games, even though he was two years older and should have been on the way to high school in Reykjavík or at sea.

She only had to show up at the football field, stock-still and pigeon-toed, and he excused himself and went to her, even though he was just about to score a goal. He abandoned everything for her. She received an electric guitar with a little amplifier as a Christmas gift from his parents, while he got an old guitar that his brother no longer bothered to practice on, some kind of children's guitar from Korea that was always going out of tune, so that he was eternally turning the pegs to increase the pitch. They sat in his room, facing each other with legs crossed, and wrote their own songs; they picked up the guitar right away and songs came naturally; they imitated one another's fingering, competing to see who would be the first to master bar chords. She sang over these chords melodies and nonmelodies with words about the wind and the absolute nothingness she found here—the constant pollution from the freezing plant, the fog, all the fucking crap. He followed her decorating the melody and quickly found the rhythm of the songs, because they were mirrors of her thoughts. They were somber songs. Except for one. She sang it at the Mass of Saint Thorlak the day before Christmas, when her father was lying on the sofa, unusually bad off and blind drunk and screaming at the world, and because she had recently learned the C-minor chord, so sweet and melancholy, she sang the song in a high-pitched and beautiful voice. It was called "Everything Will Be OK." The lyrics went like this:

Everything will be all right—will be all right
all will be all right—will be all right
I said so,
I said so

All in all will be right—will be all right
All will be all—will be all right

I said so, I said so
I said so,

I said so.

She was major and he was minor. She was stock-still and pigeon-toed, he was always going out of tune. She had brown hair with a beautiful shine that she conditioned every day with great care. He had light curls that shot out into the air and gave him a rather harmless appearance when he let his hair grow, although his intention was exactly the opposite. She was bold and audacious, but he felt like the world was always out to get them. Nobody understood them. They walked around the village, with their long hair and their dark clothes, sometimes wearing identical makeup when she felt like it, which was often. Many people thought they were smoking grass, but they didn't even know what it looked like. It was the music and the solitude, the boredom and wanderlust that set them apart from others and influenced how they behaved, talked, and dressed. Sometimes they lay together, cuddling half naked, listening to monotonous rock music thundering over their heads like a sermon. Sometimes they caressed each other's hair, cheekbones, necks, foreheads, and stroked down each other's backs. Sometimes they kissed and tasted each other's breath while caressing. She said that she loved him. He closed his eyes, squeezed them shut with all of his might, and firmly caressed her back. All around them, the kids were starting to have sex and they both knew it, but their love was different. They were different. Nobody understood them. They were going to go away as soon as they could, to where there would be music and clothes, style, words and voices—to Reykjavík, where the migratory birds of civilization spread their wings.

One morning, he came out from his room and saw his brother hanging from the crossbeam in the living room; seventeen years old, having at last decided what he was going to do with his life:

take it. In the evening, they lay half naked, cuddling, under a tall and gray sound wall while his mother talked on the phone with his father, who was out to sea. Under the sound wall, whispering between themselves, she told him how her stepfather kept trying to rub himself against her on the pretense that he needed to get something behind her, and how he was always lurking somewhere in the shadows when she was undressing for bed in the evening or took a bath—how horrible and creepy he was, and how she couldn't even tell her mom about it. Instead she had to get out of there before he became more forceful. He told her about his brother, how depressed he always was and removed and glued to his computer—and about his father, his bullying, his rage, the endless drinking when he was in dry dock. He told her about the misfortune that reigned in the house and how it finally led to the knot that was tied around his brother's neck. Together, they tried to find ten reasons life was worth living. They surrendered their pain to one another, took that pain and scrutinized it together, took care not to let it burn them. They lifted it up to the light so that it would disappear. They saw that it was ugly and lowly, but it didn't disappear.

They were sixteen years old, and nobody understood them. It was only a question of time until they could get out and do something worthwhile, meet people who weren't imbiciles. She went around in sweaters and shirts from her father, who had died when she was five years old, but Gunnar was in an Álafoss parka and black T-shirt on which a Japanese anime figure was grinding his teeth. Sometimes they wore each other's clothes, and sometimes she lined his eyes in black, and hers, too, when she felt like it, which was often, and they went out like that and walked down to the harbor and back. The world didn't stand a chance against the two of them.

How long were we together, again?

Maybe, Gunnar thinks, it sounded like I'm just making conversation about something that really doesn't matter all that much.

Maybe it sounded like everything had been just fine.

Maybe the sentence sounded like he hadn't fallen six thousand feet without a parachute and crashed hard into a kopje when she broke up with him.

Maybe it sounded like she hadn't broken both of his arms when she left him, hadn't ripped out his hair or torn off his scalp, hadn't taken his heart and stamped on it and then thrown it down to the bottom of the sea, and left him by himself at the very tip of Grímsey with open wounds for ravens to tear at.

She's sitting here across from him, looking out the window. They haven't seen each other for thirty years—since she went out and left him behind with an absence in his arms and all the words she had given him. She didn't come back, but was content to write him a letter—it was a kind letter. She's sitting here now in the kitchen next to him, and it's as if the blue chest of drawers in the corner is there only because her eyes are blue. Again, it's as if the kitchen takes its shape from her presence—its brightness from her smile. She's slipped one foot under the other like she sometimes used to, and she's looking out at Kata bicycling away.

"Who is that?" she finally asks, without answering his question, "There, on the bicycle?"

He's glad, because she's acting like nothing happened, and he starts relating the town gossip, something they had despised so deeply in the old days.

"He, Kalli from Skjol—you know, my cousin Kalli—he was in Reykjavík some years ago, as some representative, with the Valeyri Labor Union—which was really just him and Sidda, as you may remember—and then he found himself in a strip club with his friends from the labor movement . . ."

"You know, I don't want to hear this."

"No, just wait. He was down there with some fat working-class guys, watching these naked women dancing, and stuff like that, and one of the dancing girls sits down next to him, and they start talking. And you know how Kalli is, he's basically a good guy and a mechanic, and wants to solve problems like he repairs cars. He senses that she's sad and pries a rather astonishing story out of her. She was really a clarinetist, Czech or something like that, and was on her way home from an orchestra rehearsal one day when she was simply grabbed up by some thugs—right in front of her door—and they took her to a secluded spot where they pumped her full of drugs and held here there, uncared for, for weeks, and she was raped repeatedly by these criminals. So then they took her home, and she grabbed some clothes and her clarinet, and they shot her up again, and when she'd recovered her senses, she was in some whorehouse in a European city, robbed of her passport, dignity, and, basically, her future. And that's how she ended up in Reykjavík. She told all of this to Kalli, and he took it so to heart that he called Oli at the bank the day after and convinced him to finance some kind of solution. So he went to the strip club and reached an agreement with the owner to buy her contract, and she eventually ended up leading the choir, playing the organ at church, and teaching kids music. Imagine! Kalli and Sidda have since then been looking after her. Isn't this a beautiful story?"

She's still watching the woman on the bike slip away. She smiles weakly.

"Yeah, sure. But why exactly are you telling me this?"

"You know, I don't really know."

"You think he got laid?"

"No, do you really think so?"

"You're always so trusting, so naive."

She says it with a smile, and some affection comes into her voice, and he reacts as if he's never heard such praise. He pours some coffee into her cup and offers her a slice of the vínarbrauð he bought at the bakery when she called earlier and told him she was on her way. Then he pours himself a cup, and when he goes back to talking, it's in a new tone of voice, no longer lively and

impersonal. Now he's speaking in a low tone like he is telling her
something in confidence.

"And how have things been for you all these years?"

....

All these years. They went to Reykjavík together to junior college and rented a place from her aunt, who lived in an apartment
building in Solheimar. There were three bedrooms, and her aunt
gave them both room and board. They were just like her children,
and she was always trying to get them to cut their hair or get new
clothes, to read some books, watch cultured films, make something
out of themselves. They were a little embarrassed by the attention,
but also content to feel a little like twelve-year-olds. Every morning, they took the bus to school together. They sat together in class
and watched television in the evening with her aunt, who had with
great care cooked meatballs or fish steaks for them. Sometimes
she rented films by Fellini or Bergman or Woody Allen, and they
watched them with her. Sometimes they went into his room and
put up the gray sound wall and lay half naked, whispering, about
themselves and the world.

Gradually, they began noticing that the world was not one
slab, not one undivided whole before their eyes; in reality, it
consisted of countless ideas and experiences, people, colors, and
forms in a million different shades and hues. She still sometimes
came into his room with her guitar in the evening and they sat
facing each other with their legs crossed and played together, she
on the electric guitar and he with his tattered guitar from Korea
that was always going out of tune so that it became a part of the
music when he turned the pegs to increase the pitch. But now the
lyrics dealt with the strange women they had seen on the bus, and
flowers and trees and snow women. She always wore a green parka
to school, one she'd bought at the secondhand store, and he wore
a black Álafoss one and let his light hair grow out again in tangles
and harmless curls. When they started to drink, they were both

confused and out of control. They argued and tried to regain their pain from each another. They stormed off in different directions, out into the blue, until they were worn out and fell asleep in unfamiliar places, together and separately. The nights after that, they'd lie together half naked, caress each other, and hum quietly. Months passed, days, years.

They had a gig at a music evening at the school—she with her electric guitar and he with his old, unruly piece of junk—and she sang the song about how everything would be all right. Afterward, a lot of people came up to them and told them they were awesome, and after that they became a fixture of the music evenings, and the song became something of an anthem in the school, and a lot of people wanted to know them. They were open to it and became popular, because they were both mild-mannered and exciting. In the summer, they always went home and worked in the freezing plant to save enough money, even though their parents paid her aunt for their room and board. These summers boxed them in together, because here in Valeyri the world was not complex. They knew all the variations of weather, all the people, the mountain, the valley, the sea, the lake. Sometimes they went for a drive in the valley and made love there in the bottom of the valley on an Álafoss blanket in the colors of the Icelandic flag. The life in the summer revolved around fish, and they were glad when they returned to her aunt in Reykjavík, who greeted them by cooking a leg of lamb and renting *Fanny and Alexander*.

One day, he came out of physics class and saw that she was talking with some girls, and although he was her boyfriend and they were always together, he hesitated for some reason before he joined the group. When he asked her about them that evening, she said they were cool. The next day she was talking with the same girls, but now some boys had joined the group. He heard her laugh loudly, but when he looked her in the eye, her gaze told him that it wasn't a good time to join the group. They continued to sit in the same classes, but sometimes she didn't sit next to him and, gradually, they even stopped hanging around each other much during school. She started wearing white blouses and putting on perfume. He started sitting alone with her aunt and watching *Inspector Morse* and drinking tea and eating biscuits with marmalade. It was spring when they finally went to a party together to meet up with these new friends, and they both drank too much, became confused and out of control, and began to fight over their pain and stormed off separately into the night—to wherever. The girls followed after her and reached her and formed a ring around her as he wandered out into the Reykjavík night and became, once again, alone in the world. He arrived at the apartment block in Ljosheimar just before morning, and when he went inside, he saw that she hadn't returned. Maybe she was still with her friends. Maybe she wasn't. They talked about it the next day and promised each other that they would never fight again. And they would keep their promise.

They graduated in the spring. He cut his hair and let her aunt buy him new clothes, and their parents all came to Reykjavík to take part in the festivities. His father got drunk and lost for a few days, and the celebration turned into a big fuss about him. Yet the sun shone on the day they graduated. They both wore caps and had their picture taken together, holding each other. He still has the picture, framed, here in the living room—here in his summerhouse.

After graduation, he went home to work in the freezing plant, but she stayed in the town to work in a job her aunt had gotten for her. They talked on the phone every evening and gave each other words that became provisions in solicitude. She said she loved him. She said she couldn't live without him. She said she cried herself to sleep every night. He said, Yes, I know, yes, me, too. He often looked at the mountain over the town, Svarri, at its shape, and he thought that shape reflected some feeling within himself, a feeling perhaps of being left behind. He started longing to bring this shape and this sense into music. He believed that the form lived inside of him. When he told her about it, she said, Yes, exactly. I know.

He finally came to town for Jónsmessa,[1] and they went to a party with her friends in the western part of the town. They drank a lot, and all evening they sat cross-legged, facing each other with their pain in between them. She had her electric guitar and little amplifier, while he had his tattered guitar from Korea that was always going out of tune so that he was eternally turning the pegs to increase the pitch, and she sang:

Everything will be all right—will be all right
all will be all right—will be all right
I said so,
I said so

All in all will be right—will be all right
All will be all—will be all right
I said so, I said so
I said so,

I said so.

All of her friends watched them. He himself didn't have anyone in the world except her. Just before morning, they went to Thingholt as if they were lost—they weren't—and when they got to Amtmannsstígur, it was as if they had found the place that doesn't exist, the place where time doesn't exist. He always remembers that morning.

She left for university a week later, and he was left with all the words she'd said to him. He remembers them all.

---

1. An Icelandic holiday celebrated on June 24, named after John the Baptist but shrouded in folklore about elves, seals, cows, and other creatures.
—Trans.

"I've been fine," she says. "I came to bury my mother. Did you know she'd passed?"

"Yes. My condolences."

"How about you?"

"I just come to the old house in the summer sometimes to check on things and see if everything is all right. It's all I have, except for some junk in Reykjavík. What about you?"

She smiles, sets down her half-eaten slice of vínarbrauð.

"I got married. You?"

"No, I'm single. I teach music. You?"

"Me, too. Do you want to know more about me?"

"No. Sure. I don't really know."

"Maybe we should take a walk?" she asks.

"Yes, absolutely," he says nervously. They stand up, slip on their coats, and he holds the door for her on the way out. He slides his other hand into his pocket. There he has the harmonica.

Translated by Meg Matich

The Universe and the Deep Velvet Dress

JÓN KALMAN STEFÁNSSON

1

O NE NIGHT HE STARTED TO DREAM IN LATIN. *Tu igitur nihil vidis?* Although it was long unclear which language it was, he himself believed that it had come alive on its own, dreams pregnant with meaning, and so forth. In those years, looking around the village was quite different. We moved a little more slowly, and the cooperative held everything together. He was, however, the CEO of the Wool Company, newly turned thirty. He had the world at his feet and had married such a beautiful woman that some people felt peculiar inside when they saw her; they had two children, and we assume that one of them, David, will yet emerge in the story on these pages. The young CEO seemed born to victory. The family lived in the biggest house in the village, he drove a Range Rover, his suits were tailor-made, we all paled in comparison, but then he began to dream in Latin. It was the old doctor who eventually decided on the language, but, unfortunately, he died shortly afterward, when Guðjón's mongrel lunged at him, barking, and his old heart gave out. We shot the goddamn dog immediately the next day, although it could've been sooner. Guðjón threatened a lawsuit but then got another dog that was far worse; some of us have tried to run it over, but the scoundrel is quick on his feet. All the same, the old doctor knew next to nothing in Latin, just a few words and the names of organs, but that was enough when the CEO finally managed to memorize the sentence in his dream.

No one who starts dreaming in Latin is woven from everyday materials. English, Danish, German, yeah, sure, French, and even Spanish, it's good to know something in those languages; they enlarge one's internal world, after all. But Latin, that's something else entirely. It's so much bigger that we can scarcely trust ourselves to describe it further. But the CEO was a man who got things done, nothing stopped him. He wanted to have control over everything around him, and it was so damn irritating to him that the dreams were filled with this language he couldn't understand at all. There was only one thing to be done about it—travel to the south for two months of intensive private lessons in Latin.

He was so gallant, almost unscrupulous, in those years. He drove south in the Range Rover. He'd bought a new Toyota Corolla, an automatic, for his wife, so that she didn't overexert her beautiful and slender legs while he was in the south. Still, it was rather gratuitous to buy a car for her, because people had willingly driven her around the streets in the village during every stage of her life; but he drove south in his tailor-made suit, his expression determined but impatient, the confidence in his demeanor deep-seated, although, of course, we can't be sure. Peaceful dreams, resembling a vast lake, spread out around him, and the boat was waiting for him at shore.

2

WE WOULD LIKE TO GET AN EXPLANATION, or explanations, for the great conversion, metamorphosis even, that the CEO underwent. He went south and came back radically transformed, a man who had come closer to heaven than to earth. Yes, he came back from the south fluent in Latin; it threw us for a loop, but we didn't notice the metamorphosis immediately. He still had the

Range Rover, but his clothes were starting to look the worse for wear, his voice was lower, his movements slower, and it was as if the man had been given new eyes. The steadfast gaze was gone. In its place came something that we hardly knew the name of, maybe absentmindedness, maybe dreaminess; and at the same time it was as if he saw through everything, all of it, all of the bustle and the small talk and the noise that characterize our lives, all of the fuss about weight, finance, wrinkles, politics, hairdressers. Maybe we should've all gone south to learn Latin and gotten a new pair of eyes; then our village would probably launch into the air and float up in the sky. But we absolutely can't go, of course. You know how it is, firmly stuck in the magnetic field of habit, which was how it usually was, the sleep-inducing song of the everyday that acclimated us—astonishingly quickly—to his new eyes, the tattered clothes, the changes in his demeanor. People are always changing, getting new hobbies, coloring their hair, cheating, dying; it's hopeless to keep track of all of it, and we have enough on our plates, learning about the noise in our own heads. But more than a year after the CEO's Latin course, a package arrived at the post office from abroad. The box was labeled CAUTION in nine languages. Augusta, a post office employee, was so taken aback that she didn't dare open the box, and we had to wait quite a few days to find out what was in it. As you can imagine, there were predictions and speculations, there were diverse theories, which proved, however, to be far off, because it was only a book in the box, albeit an old and famous book, The Starry Messenger by Galileo Galilei. It was an original edition that was not small, because the book had been printed around four hundred years ago. It was written in Latin, and in one place is this sentence:

But forsaking terrestrial observations, I turned to celestial ones.

It's not easy to better describe the changes in our CEO, or Astronomer, as someone called him after examining the contents of the package; his namesake was the old eccentric who had died many years ago. No doubt the CEO was thought a laughingstock, and the name immediately stuck to him. His disgrace grew quickly alongside the name. It was actually his wife who told us about the book. She seemed to have a great need to explain how different her husband had become, and you can believe that there were many ready to listen. She often used black lipstick, and if only you could've seen her in her green sweater, so beautiful, so graceful. She lived in our dreams, and some people—Simmi, for example, who was a bachelor nearing fifty, a great horseman, had twelve horses, was downright obsessed with her and sometimes thought of moving away to get some balance in his life. He went out riding every day and was frequently spotted in front of her house, hoping to catch a glimpse of her if only for a split second. And one day Simmi got on a brown horse, rode out, and saw her hurrying out of the house.

He first turned in a wide curve so that he was riding toward her, and they met, she with those black lips, that delicate face, red hair, nose just like a tear, eyes so blue, and she was in a green sweater under a loose jacket, beautiful, even a revelation, and nobody knows exactly how it happened, but Simmi, this highly experienced horseman, fell off the animal's back. Beauty made me fall from my horse, is what he'd say later on, but some believed that he had simply thrown himself from the horse in a sort of despair or momentary fit of madness. He broke his femur, fractured his leg, and there he lay. No doctor in the village. The old doctor had died three days earlier, goddamn dog, goddamn Guðjón, and no hope of a new one for at least a week. We were directed to maintain our health in the meantime—those with heart disease were to stay put—but then Simmi fell off the back of the horse. She ran over to him, gave him first aid, her eyes bluer than anything else. There was some discussion of sending him south to a hospital, but we really dislike bother and commotion, and the veterinarian was a good enough substitute; Simmi just limped around that day. Those moments, when she knelt over him and he breathed in her sweet and warm scent, are the best and most precious in his life, moments he goes over in his head again and again. It is, however, unlikely that she would care to live the events again, as she had newly discovered that her husband had exchanged the Range Rover, and the Toyota, too, for *The Starry Messenger* by Galileo. He thought it was a self-explanatory thing; didn't even feel like talking about it. Most horribly of all, she rushed out, furious and so desperate that she barely caught her breath. The world had started crumbling around her, and then this horseman showed up out of nowhere. It must tear something asunder inside of you, for example, the heartstrings, when the person whom you believe you know down to the letter, who enraptured you, married you, had children with you, and a home, and memories, stands one day in front of you a complete stranger. As a matter of fact, it's sheer nonsense to believe that you know someone down to the letter; there are always dark corners in the mind, and that's all fine and good. She was married to a relatively young man with connections in the community, the very pillars of the village, a man who had an influence on our lives. A business with little hope flourished under his leadership and turned a profit. He was a paragon. He was hope and an anchor, but then he started to dream in Latin, drove south to learn the language, returned with new eyes, and sold their cars a year later to pay for old books. In comparison with all of this, one man falling off his horse is trivial, but we're only talking about the very beginning.

The days rose up in the east, they vanished into the west, the Astronomer was hardly seen at the Wool Company, and Augusta left the post office more than a few times to go over to the married couple's mansion with new packages, some marked CAUTION in nine languages. Three or four weeks after the Italian Galileo freed the married couple of two cars, the Astronomer received an even older book, *On the Revolutions of the Heavenly Spheres* by Copernicus, printed in the year 1543. It cost every penny they had—the mansion was only just enough to buy it—but her patience, which some miss so sorely, finally gave out when he received first editions of Johannes Kepler's seventeenth-century *Rudolphine Tables, Harmony of the Worlds*, and *The Dreamer: Posthumous Work on Lunar Astronomy*. Even before they arrived at the post office, many tried to bring the Astronomer to his senses: the head of the bank, the magistrate, the school principal, a delegate from the staff at the Wool Company. The people asked him, What are you doing with your life, throwing it away on books, you're emptying your accounts, losing your house, you're losing your very life, get a grip, good man! But it was all in vain. He just looked at the people with these new eyes of his and he felt compassion for them and said something in Latin that nobody understood. It's needless to report that he carried on; at least fifteen years have passed, and he now has about three thousand books and counting. They cover the walls of his little house, many of them in Latin just like those that had freed him from beauty, comfort, and domesticity.

Shortly after Augusta delivered the package with the Kepler books, his wife moved south with their daughter. David was, however, left with his father, who bought a two-story timber house overlooking the main cluster of houses in the village. It had been unoccupied since old Bogga died in her bunk and nobody knew until the direction of the wind changed and the stench blew from the house over to the dairy farm, which was also isolated from the little village. When the Astronomer bought the house, it looked like an old, worn-out horse, half blind and dying, but he replaced the rotting timber with new wood, the cracked windows with new panes. Just consider whether it would be very easy to update a rotting worldview, a dying culture. Then he painted the house coal black, outside of a few white drops on three sides and the roof. The drops are four constellations that he has the most fondness for: the Big Dipper, the Seven Sisters, Cassiopeia, and the Herdsman. The fourth side is black. It faces to the west and toward the sea and represents the end of the world. It's not especially uplifting, but the western wall faces away from the road. The Astromoner's house is the first one visitors see when they come to the village from the southern valleys; in the daytime, it's just like fragments fallen from the night sky to the earth and into the village. There is a big window that opens on the roof of the house, and late in the evening, a telescope pokes out, a single eye that takes in distance, dark, and light. He now lives alone in the house—David moved to the village at seventeen—and sometimes he listens to the creaking of distant windows as winter darkness tightens around them.

Translated by Meg Matich

Contributors

Following Icelandic custom, authors are alphabetized by first name.

ÁGÚST BORGÞÓR SVERRISSON is a leading short story writer in Iceland and has published in magazines and literary journals as well as his five books of short stories. His most recent book is a psychological thriller. He works as a journalist and copywriter.

ANDRI SNÆR MAGNASON has won the Icelandic Literary Award in all three categories: fiction, nonfiction, and YA. He is the author of the Philip K. Dick Award–winning sci-fi novel *LoveStar*. He codirected the documentary film *Dreamland,* and his children's book and play adaptation *The Story of the Blue Planet* has been published or performed in thirty-five countries.

AUÐUR AVA ÓLAFSDÓTTIR lives in Reykjavík. She studied art history in Paris and taught art history and theory at the University of Iceland. She has written four novels, a book of poetry, and four plays. Her novels *The Greenhouse* and *Butterflies* have been translated into English, and she received Le Prix littéraire des Jeunes Européens, as well as other national and international literary awards.

AUÐUR JÓNSDÓTTIR is one of the most accomplished authors writing in Icelandic today. Since 1998 she has published seven novels, two children's books, one screenplay based on one of her novels, and many essays for Icelandic as well as international publications. She won the Icelandic Literary Prize for *The People in the Basement* and the Icelandic

Women's Literature Prize for *Secretaries to the Spirits*. Both novels were nominated for the Nordic Council Literary Prize. Her novels are recognized in Iceland as well as abroad for their rare blend of incisive candor and humor.

BRAGI ÓLAFSSON is the author of seven novels and several books of poetry, short stories, and plays. Two of his novels, *The Pets* and *The Ambassador*, have been published in the United States, and *Narrator* is forthcoming. He has translated poetry from Spanish and French, as well as a novel by Paul Auster, *City of Glass*, and two plays by Harold Pinter for the National Theater of Iceland, *The Birthday Party* and *The Homecoming*. He lives in Reykjavík.

EINAR MÁR GUÐMUNDSSON has published thirteen novels, two collections of short stories, and eight collections of poetry. His books have been translated into several languages. He received the Nordic Council Literature Prize in 1995 for *Angels of the Universe*, a novel that was later adapted into a successful film.

EINAR ÖRN GUNNARSSON has published four novels and many short stories. His play *The Crow's Palace* has been performed, and his novel *The Tears of the Bird of Paradise* was published in translation.

GERÐUR KRISTNÝ has received numerous awards for her nonfiction as well as her children's books, novels, and poetry. Her poetry is recognized internationally and has been translated into thirty languages. For her modern rewriting of Norse myths, the poetic cycle *Bloodhoof*, she received the Icelandic Literature Award and was nominated for the Nordic Council Award.

GUÐMUNDUR ANDRI THORSSON graduated from the University of Iceland, where he studied literary theory and Icelandic studies. He is editor of the Icelandic literary magazine *TMM* and has written several novels and short stories. His book *The Valeyri Waltz* has been published in Denmark, Norway, Germany, and France.

GYRÐIR ELÍASSON has published seven novels and numerous collections of short stories and poetry. His writing has been published in translation in Germany, France, England, and Scandinavia. He received the Nordic Council Literature Prize in 2011.

HELEN MITSIOS is professor of languages and literature at Touro College and University System in New York City. She is the editor of several literature anthologies, including *Beneath the Ice: An Anthology of Contemporary Icelandic Poetry* and *Digital Geishas and Talking Frogs: The Best Twenty-first Century Short Stories from Japan*. Her collection *New Japanese Voices: The Best Contemporary Fiction from Japan* was listed as an Editors' Choice and Summer Reading Selection by the *New York Times Book Review*. She is coauthor of *Waltzing with the Enemy: A Mother and Daughter Confront the Aftermath of the Holocaust* and author of the poetry collection *If Black Had a Shadow*.

JÓN KALMAN STEFÁNSSON has published several collections of poetry, short stories, and ten novels. His best-known work is a trilogy of novels: *Heaven and Hell*, *The Sorrow of Angels*, and *The Heart of Man*. Three of his books have been nominated for the Nordic Council Literature Prize. His writing has been translated into German, French, English, and the Scandinavian languages.

KRISTÍN EIRÍKSDÓTTIR has published four books of poetry; a collection of short stories, *Doris Dies*; and the novel *Hvítfeld—A Family Saga*. With Kari Ósk Grétudóttir she cowrote the play *Karma for Birds*, which was performed at Iceland's National Theater and nominated for best play of the year for the Gríman, Iceland's theater award. The Reykjavík City Theater staged her play *Hystory in 2015*, also nominated for best play of the year for the Gríman. Her stories and poems have been translated into Danish, German, and English.

KRISTÍN ÓMARSDÓTTIR has published six novels, three books of short stories, and seven books of poetry. Her plays have been produced for the stage, and her novels have been translated into many languages, including Swedish, French, and English. She won Iceland's Gríman Playwright of the Year Award in 2005, as well as other literature awards and honors.

MAGNÚS SIGURÐSSON is a poet and translator. His awards include the 2008 Tómas Guðmundsson Literary Prize for his debut collection of poems and the 2013 Jón úr Vör Poetry Prize. Among his translations into Icelandic are Ezra Pound's *The Pisan Cantos* and a selection of Adelaide Crapsey's poems. *Cold Moons*, a book of poems translated into English, is forthcoming.

ÓLAFUR GUNNARSSON is author of fifteen novels, two collections of short stories, poetry, and children's books. His novel *Trolls' Cathedral* was adapted for the stage for Iceland's National Theater. He was awarded the Icelandic Literature Prize in 2003. His writing has been translated into several languages, and his children's book *The Beautiful Flying Whale* has been published internationally.

ÓSKAR ÁRNI ÓSKARSSON was editor and publisher of the Icelandic literary magazine *Ský* from 1990 until 1994. His translations include three books of Japanese haiku and *The Ballad of the Sad Café* by Carson McCullers. His poetry collection *Silhouettes of a Journey*, based on autobiographical memories, was nominated for the Icelandic Literary Prize. Most recently he has written the poetry books *Three Hands*, *Conch Museum*, and *The Tin Angel*.

ÓSKAR MAGNÚSSON holds law degrees from the University of Iceland and George Washington University in Washington, D.C. He has published two collections of short stories, *Did I Eat Supper Last Night?* and *I Cannot See a Thing without My Glasses*, and the novels *Let's Lower Down Chaps* and *The Defense Attorney*. He is known in the Icelandic business world as a news editor, a Supreme Court attorney, a CEO of prominent enterprises, and a newspaper and website publisher.

RÚNAR VIGNISSON is an Icelandic author and translator. He has won the Icelandic Translation Award for J. M. Coetzee's *Boyhood* and has translated books by American, English, and Australian authors such as Philip

Roth, Amy Tan, William Faulkner, Ian McEwan, and Elizabeth Jolley. He is the author of four novels and three collections of short stories, and for his fiction he has been shortlisted for the Icelandic Literature Award and has won the DV Cultural Prize for Literature. His short stories have been translated into Spanish, German, Polish, Chinese, and English. He is director of the Creative Writing Program at the University of Iceland.

SJÓN is an award-winning author and poet. His novels *The Blue Fox, The Whispering Muse, From the Mouth of the Whale,* and *Moonstone: The Boy Who Never Was* have been translated into thirty-five languages. He has published nine poetry collections and written four opera librettos and lyrics for several artists. In 2001 he was nominated for an Academy Award for his lyrics in the film *Dancer in the Dark.* He is president of the Icelandic PEN Centre and lives in Reykjavík.

ÞÓRUNN ERLU-VALDIMARSDÓTTIR has written more than twenty books, including novels, poetry, short stories, biographies, and scholarly works, as well as programs for radio and television. Her novels *Cold Blood* and *The Lion Has Many Ears* are contemporary crime stories based on the sagas Njála and Laxdæla.

ÞÓRARINN ELDJÁRN studied in Iceland and Sweden. He published his first collection of poetry in 1974 and has since published many books of poetry and children's verse, as well as short stories and novels. He has translated books and plays into Icelandic from English and Scandinavian languages by authors such as Lewis Carroll, Shakespeare, August Strindberg, and Henrik Ibsen.